RAVENWOOD ACADEMY

Wolf Moon

Ravenwood Academy

Year One

Lena Mae Hill

Chapter One

"Hey, Dracula," said a voice behind me as I walked out of class.

"Hey, peanut," I shot back.

Dale fought the tide of students to catch up because today just happened to be my lucky day. "Peanut? Where did that come from?"

"You know, your nickname. Because I hear you're hung like a peanut."

His fists clenched. "What? Where'd you hear that?"

"I just heard it from you, dumbass," I said with my sweetest smile. "When you didn't deny it."

His eyes widened, the vein in his throat bulging. "You bitch."

"No, no," I said, then did my best Tarzan imitation. "Me, Timberlyn. You Dale."

"Huh?" he asked, obviously not appreciating my sparkling humor.

I sighed. "Don't worry, I'm sure you're at least as big as a circus peanut."

"Fucking dyke," he snarled, his eyes narrowing.

Yes, I lived in a small town. There were lovely people in the town, but I went to the kind of school where the fact that I wore all black made me a dyke, and the fact that I drew monsters in my notebook made me a target of assholes like Dale.

I made it to my locker, where Lindy stood rifling through her books. For the third year in a row, I had managed to trade lockers with someone and get one next to hers. That might sound stalkerish, but I preferred to call it my natural curiosity and an active imagination.

I'd met Lindy three years ago when she moved to our Podunk town—a year after I'd had my first dream about her. I didn't always dream about monsters, though that was more common than regular people. Lindy could be called nothing if not regular, though. After she'd appeared out of my dream, I'd begun studying her, determined to find out what was special about her. Three years later, I still didn't know why she'd appeared to me before I met her.

"Hey, girl," I said, giving her a bright smile as I opened my locker. Since I spent most of my day perfecting my Resting Bitch Face so people would think twice before messing with me, it felt strange to relax.

Lindy returned my smile with a bland one of her own. Considering how long we'd been locker neighbors, you might think that we'd become friends. But the truth was, neither of us had any friends—not even each other. I'd tried to talk to Lindy for years, but she was either the best, most secretly badass poker player of all time, or she'd been born with a rare genetic condition that consisted of a complete absence of personality. I was halfway convinced she was a secret government spy. Or maybe a robot. One day, when the truth came out, I could say "Hey, I used to talk to the famous Lindy Johnson."

Still, I did my best to be friendly and chase away the assholes when they dropped by. Today we made our way to class without further harassment and dropped into our seats. Alyvia made a face like I smelled bad and scooted her desk a few inches away.

Though this was not unusual, I ducked my head and did a quick pit-check. No one wanted to smell like B.O.

Alyvia looked me up and down from the corner of her eye. "Could you be more tacky?"

"I could try," I said.

"And your friend," she said, cutting her eyes toward Lindy. "Didn't she wear that outfit yesterday?"

When Lindy had moved here, she hadn't even attracted the male attention that most new girls did. New kids were usually a novelty for a few months in our small town, but instead, Lindy had quickly become a target of the mean girls because of her appearance. When I had gotten a locker beside hers, it had become one of my personal missions to stick up for her since she didn't do it for herself. Despite what the girls said, her style wasn't bad. It kinda matched her surface personality. She mostly wore generic sneakers, oversized t-shirts that hid her shape, and no-name jeans. I didn't really care what she wore or what personality she had. I just wanted to know why I had dreamed about her. Somewhere under that bland exterior, she had to be hiding something. Maybe she was a serial killer plotting all our deaths. I did dream of monsters, after all.

Hopefully she'd spare me since I'd stood up for her all these years. That's how it always worked in fairytales. You were supposed to be nice to people no matter what they looked like. Otherwise, you could be turned into the beast, and no girl needed that back hair situation.

I gave Lindy about ten seconds to answer Alyvia, hoping this would be the day when she'd finally decide to speak up. Instead, she slumped down in her desk like she was trying to disappear.

"Leave Lindy out of this, or I'll curse you," I hissed, waving my fingers at the mean girl. "I'm a witch, after all."

"Whatever, freak," Alyvia said, flicking her hair back.

"That hair you love to swish around so much is going to get all brittle and fall out if you keep messing with Lindy," I hissed. "Every single hair will turn into a split end."

"Oh my God, leave me alone," she said, looking actually scared now.

I turned away, rolling my eyes. Once, I might have been friends with girls like her. But I'd made the mistake of being myself once in middle school and telling the truth about my drawings. One of my friends had asked how I could draw monsters with such detail, where I came up with such things. When I'd told her I saw them in my dreams, she'd gone around telling everyone that I dreamed of being a monster when I grew up. Dumb, yes, but it had worked. It didn't take much to stand out in middle school, and not in a good way.

Since then, I'd been the freaky monster girl. And as the saying went, if you can't convince them otherwise, you might as well be the freak they think you are. Or something along those lines.

The truth was, I didn't want to be friends with those girls. I just wanted to go to a school where you could be something besides popular or a loser. Sure, at first it had hurt being cast into the loser role, but everything hurt in sixth grade. By the next year I had learned to lace up my big girl boots, march into school like I didn't give a fuck, and ignore the bitches. At night, I'd applied for private schools all over the country to get me out of this Podunk little town before high school started. Needless to say, I hadn't been accepted to a single one.

My parents didn't make a lot of money, so I needed a scholarship. But I wasn't particularly gifted, and my grades were only average. The schools I applied to sent back polite form letters telling me that I wasn't quite the candidate their school had in mind. So, here I was, in October of my freshman year, still dreaming of monsters by night and facing a different kind of monster by day.

As I walked out of class with Lindy, I looked up to see Dale coming toward us again. Apparently, I was so scary I warranted a small army, and he'd recruited them between his classroom and mine.

"Looks like we're about to get a visit from the goon squad," I said to Lindy as they approached.

"Hey, dykes."

I turned to Lindy. "Did I tell you I started a fan club? Here they are."

"You wish, Timberloony," Dale said. "I just wanted to know what you're dressing up as for Halloween. You're already scary the other 365 days of the year. Does that mean you're going to look normal for one day?"

"Actually, that would be 364 days," I said.

Dale looked confused by my math, but instead of trying to wrap his head around it, he turned his attention to the two mean girls who had just arrived. Alyvia preened under his gaze, but she joined right in the conversation. "What about you, Lindy? What are you going to dress up as—plain oatmeal?"

Dale and his friends burst out laughing like that was actually funny. It was wittier than anything Dale could come up with, so I couldn't blame him.

"No, no," said Amanda. "She's going to dress up as a dirty dish towel."

"She already wears that every day," Alyvia said.

"Didn't I tell you to mind your own business or your hair would fall out?" I said. "And Dale, can't you find someone your own size to pick on?"

"You mean like you?" Amanda asked. Their group started laughing like they thought that was the best burn ever.

"Well, I don't know if I'm as big as Dale all over," I said. "But I know one place I am."

"Why don't you just go as Dyke One and Dyke Two?" Dale asked.

"Y'all can make me into a Timber-Lindy sandwich," said his friend. "I'll even let you grind on me. You know, a pity dance."

"As much fun as that sounds, I think I'll be staying home to draw monsters," I said. "I'd rather not have to dance with them as well as see them in my dreams."

I'd long ago stopped trying to explain away my weirdness and embraced it whole hog. Hence the black lipstick and combat boots.

Timberlyn dreams of monsters.

9

Timberlyn draws monsters.

Timberlyn is a monster.

Dracula.

Frankenstein.

Freak.

While I'd engaged in this stimulating debate, Lindy had closed her locker and scurried off. When she'd disappeared out the doors to the safety of whatever waited for her at home, I finally said my goodbyes.

"Have fun at the dance," I said, turning and heading for the exit. "Don't get pregnant."

With that, I pushed out the doors, forcing them open against the raging wind. The moist air dampened my face as the wind whipped my hair into my mouth. Thick, blue-black storm clouds writhed overhead. I headed down the steps and started for home, pulling my black leather jacket closed around myself. Despite my mother's fretting, I refused to take the bus, preferring the mile walk instead.

It wasn't just that the bus was a hell that any sane person avoided. These twenty minutes were my comfort and solace each day. Despite not having friends, I got more than enough attention at school. Here, walking on the empty sidewalks, I could let my guard down. I didn't have to be badass Timberlyn who didn't give a shit what anyone thought of her. I wasn't the freak, the protector of Lindy, or even the good daughter who had plenty of friends at school. I didn't have to be anyone. I was just me.

Just Timberlyn, the girl who saw creatures in her dreams that wouldn't leave her alone until she drew them. The girl who had applied to every private school in the country and struck out every time. The girl who was still determined to get the hell out of this town at the first opportunity, even if she had no idea how that was going to happen.

Chapter Two

I stood at the mailbox, staring down at the oversized envelope clutched in my hand. The wind threatened to yank it from my hands and sent leaves skating along the pavement. My heart hammered erratically in my chest as I reread the return address.

Ravenwood Academy for the Exceptionally Gifted.

There must be a mistake. Though I'd applied to a hundred schools like this, they'd all rejected me by June at the latest. Now, four months since the last letter arrived, I was holding a thick envelope from a school I didn't even remember applying to, with the familiar sense of dread and desperate hope battling it out in my stomach.

Exceptionally gifted? I tried to remember what I could have sent this school in an attempt to convince them I was worthy. I was no more likely to get into an art school for drawing monsters than Stephen King was to win a Pulitzer for writing about them. As far as other gifts… I was exceptionally persistent in trying to figure out my dreams. I was exceptionally good at hiding pain behind snark and sarcasm. I had an exceptional number of black outfits in my closet. Were those gifts?

A fat drop of rain pelted onto the envelope as if to punctuate my ridiculous thought. I glanced up at the sky just as an ominous rumble of thunder sounded, and another drop of rain bit into my cheek like it had a personal vendetta.

Tucking the envelope inside my jacket, I jogged up the walkway and through the front door. I wanted to toss the envelope on the counter and tell myself it was nothing. If they were this late sending out letters, it had to be a rejection. But why was the envelope so thick, so squishy?

I fought for a breath as I stood at the counter, trying in vain not to get my hopes up.

"Timberlyn?" my sister called from the living room, where I could hear the soothing sound of her vintage Super Mario video game. "Wanna play?"

"Yeah," I said, wiping my damp red hair off my forehead and looking down at the envelope in my hands. It was better just to get it over with. Otherwise I'd spend all night thinking about it.

In one motion I ripped open the top of the envelope and dumped the contents onto the counter. A letter slid out, along with a folded T-shirt.

Why would I get a T-shirt if…

I couldn't finish the thought. With shaking hands, I dove for the letter, flattening it and scanning the words with disbelief, going back to the first word over and over.

Congratulations!

Congratulations.

Oh my god.

Congratulations!

My fingers were numb as I picked up the T-shirt and shook it out. It was soft and grey, with the word Ravenwood printed across the chest in simple teal letters.

"What's that?"

My sister had come into the room while I was occupied, and now I turned to her, my heart racing. "It's... From a school," I said. "I think... I think I got in."

I couldn't stop the smile from spreading over my face or the tears from blurring my eyes.

"Really?" Josie asked. "Cool. Where's it at?"

"I don't know," I said. "I don't remember. I don't even remember applying there." Actually, I'd never heard of the school in my life. I was sure of it. Suddenly, a heavy, sick feeling started to form in the pit of my stomach. How official was a T-shirt that just had a word on the front? Shouldn't it have an official-looking seal?

Yes, I'd applied to too many schools to count. But I'd recognize the name of any one of them. I could have told you what state they were in at the very least. The name Ravenwood didn't even sound familiar.

My backpack hit the floor with a thud, and I bent to dig through it, pulling out a battered composition notebook. I flipped it open to the list of schools I'd spent the last year writing down, checking off when I sent my application, and then, one by one, crossing out. There were a few that had never bothered to write back at all, so they had been spared my black Sharpie. I ran my finger down the page checking the schools that hadn't outright rejected me.

There was no Ravenwood Academy anywhere on my list. Not even when I squinted to read the ones I'd crossed out. I had pretty much resigned myself to going to Podunk High for the rest of my life, but this one taste of hope… It was worse than never hoping at all. The cruelty of it made my eyes blur over with tears for a different reason.

"Well?" Josie asked. "Where's Ravenwood?"

"Nowhere," I said, slamming my notebook shut and sucking in a long, slow breath, hoping my sister didn't see my tears. "I'm not going. It's not a real school."

Someone at school must have looked in my notebook when I was out of my seat at some point. They'd seen the list of schools I wanted to go to, and they'd thought it would be fun to make me think I was gifted at something other than not fitting in.

But who would do that? Sure, people were assholes, but who hated me this much? Who would be so cruel they'd create this elaborate hoax just to crush my spirit?

"Can I have the shirt, then?" Josie asked, holding the T-shirt up to her preteen form. "I like it."

"Sure, whatever," I said, crumbling the paper and tossing it in the recycling bin.

"Who sent it, anyway?" she asked, pulling it over her head and tugging her red hair from the neck of it.

"I don't know," I said. "I guess somebody who thought it would be funny."

Somebody who had a seriously sick sense of humor. Anger welled inside me as I thought about it, about what kind of person would look through my personal, private notebook, figure out what I was doing, and see my desperation to escape this town. Then they'd gone to all the trouble to print a shirt? I didn't know I was that important to anyone, that they'd hate me that much. Well, they might have thought it was funny, but it wasn't. And they'd just made themselves an enemy. Because when I found out who sent that letter, they were going to pay.

Chapter Three

"Got big plans for Halloween?" Dad asked, his salt and pepper mustache waggling as he spoke in his usual big, blustering voice.

"I'm sure Josie wants to go trick-or-treating. Don't you, sweetie?" Mom asked, patting my sister's hand and giving her a saccharine smile.

"Mom, I'm twelve," Josie said, rolling her eyes and giving me a look that said I better help her. Since she'd probably blab about the Ravenwood prank if I didn't, I jumped in.

"I can't take her this year," I said. In truth, I hated Halloween, though I pretended to love it at school.

Everyone thought I was an actual monster, after all. I had to play that up for any advantage when I could.

"Why not, dear?" Mom asked. "Can you pass the salt, please?"

I handed her the salt. "I'm busy."

As soon as the words were out, I cringed. Crap. Now they were going to ask about my plans, and I'd have to make up something and stay out of the house all evening on Halloween, anyway. I might as well go trick-or-treating with my sister.

"That's fine, honey," Dad said, patting my hand with his thick, red fingers. "You go on and have fun with your friends." He winked at me like we were in on some big secret, which I hoped didn't mean he'd finally figured out that I had no friends. If he did, though, he'd never let on.

Around the time everyone else realized I was a freak, my parents must have had a secret meeting and decided a preteen girl was the scariest thing in the world. Ever since then, they'd treated me like a grenade they were waiting to blow up. I'd noticed them start to treat Josie the same way over the past year. Or maybe they treated us like a panel of judges as they tried out for their starring roles as Mom and Dad. Either way, it was exhausting. Not only did they act like they were performing, but it forced us to participate in the charade of our lives.

"I suppose we could skip this one year if you both have parties to attend," Mom said. "But surely you need costumes."

"I don't need one," I said.

"That's right," Dad boomed. "Timberlyn wears a costume every day."

"Ooh, burn," Josie said.

I kicked her under the table. "For your information, a boy asked me to the Halloween dance," I said, already feeling guilty for the deception. It wasn't exactly a lie, though. Someone really had said he'd dance with me. I just didn't mention that it had been a taunt.

"That's great, sweetheart," Mom said, patting my other hand. My parents were big on the hand-patting.

"Who's this boy?" Dad asked. "Do I need to show him my shotgun?" He gave me another wink, and my sister and I rolled our eyes in unison.

"No, we're just going as friends," I rushed to say. That's what happened when I lied. More lies became necessary. Now I just wanted to backpedal and tell the truth, but I couldn't bear the thought of breaking my parents' hearts with the truth. If they were content to live in their delusion, who was I to ruin their happiness?

"Well, I'm glad you're getting out with your friends," Mom said. "Sometimes I worry about you. All that black you wear. Are you depressed, dear?"

Oh, god.

"Mom," Josie said with a groan. "Clothes are a form of self-expression. That doesn't mean she's depressed."

"Well, if you ask me, all that black makes you unapproachable," Mom said. "Can't you express something more cheerful? Your red hair would look so pretty with a yellow blouse."

"Can I be excused?" I asked, pushing back from the table and escaping before Mom could throw me in a ruffled romper like I was two years old. My combat boots thudded up the stairs as I climbed to my room. Whether or not they were a form of self-expression, my boots were part of me.

I flopped down across my bed. My bed with yellow ruffles.

I rolled over onto my back to escape the horror.

The ceiling seemed lower every day, as if the house were trying to smother me. This place wasn't my refuge. It was just one more place that where I didn't fit, one more place that wanted me to be something I wasn't.

I sat up and swung my legs over the edge of the bed. Opening my laptop, I typed the words into the search bar before I could second guess myself.

Ravenwood Academy for the Exceptionally Gifted.

To my surprise, a legitimate website popped up. Heart pounding, I scrolled down the page. The backdrop showed an old-fashioned sort of building I associated more with a university than a high school. There was only one page, but it looked… Real.

I could barely breathe as I searched again, looking for reviews on other sites. I found only two reviews, one of them saying it was the first school where the student had ever felt accepted and at home. Back on the school's website, I read the description, which described small classes, a rigorous curriculum, and a chance for students to discover and develop their natural gifts.

My heart raced as I grabbed up my laptop and ran downstairs. My sister had retired to her room, but my parents were watching Late Night in the living room.

"Mom?" I said, scooting in beside her. "Remember when we applied for all those private schools last year?"

"Of course, honey," she said, glancing at my screen. "Did you want to apply to another one for next year?"

"No, I…" I started, then shook my head. "Did you apply to this one? Ravenwood?"

"I don't remember the name," she said, frowning at the TV. "I could check my spreadsheet. Where is it?"

I scrolled down again, drawing back when I saw the address. "It's… In Canada. Vancouver Island. Where Grandma lives."

That got Mom's attention. "I did tell her about our search last year," she mused, a frown creasing her brow. "Do you think she filled out an application?"

I felt as doubtful as Mom looked. I wasn't sure my grandmother had joined the digital age. "Maybe," I said slowly. "She could have done it late, and that's why we're just hearing from them now."

I was just looking for any excuse to go, to believe it. Maybe that made me desperate, but then, who was I kidding? I was more than a little desperate. I was tired of playacting my life. I wanted to live it. If someone had told me my unicorn was parked outside waiting to whisk me away, I would've run right out. Hell, I wouldn't even run upstairs for my beloved combat boots.

"Well, let's give her a call," Mom said, since she wasn't quite up for unicorn riding yet. Despite her disapproval of my life choices—and by that, I mean my wardrobe—she did love me. I loved my family, too. I just didn't fit them. They'd all be more comfortable with me gone, except maybe Josie. And she was adaptable, fitting easily into the middle ground between me and my parents. Without me there, she wouldn't have to be a buffer for their criticism of me.

After chatting a few minutes, Mom handed me the phone, and I stepped into the kitchen so Dad wouldn't have to hear the TV over my voice.

"Hey, Gramma," I said.

"Your mother tells me you're going to Ravenwood," she said, her voice high but gravelly, with a slight quaver that had come with age.

"I actually wasn't sure it was a real place," I admitted, taking a seat at the island.

"Oh, it's real alright," Gramma said. "I've seen it with my own two eyes. Now, they're not what they used to be, but I still see well enough to know that much."

"Did you apply for me to go there?" I asked. "I don't think I did, and Mom doesn't remember, either."

Gramma paused a second. "I don't recall, Timberlyn. My memory's not what it used to be, either, you know. But it's a wonderful school. You should come and visit if you're unsure, but I hear nothing but good things about it. Unlike these woods behind my house... I hear all kinds of things from there."

I didn't know how to answer that. Gramma's memory was spotty, and sometimes her mind seemed to drift to some other time or place without warning. Mom had tried to get her to let someone move in to take care of her, but Gramma had vehemently refused.

But maybe…

I saw it all so clearly. I could help Gramma when she needed it, check in on her without making her feel smothered like an invalid. She was still strong and capable in most things, but it wouldn't hurt to have someone there to visit on weekends, make sure she got help if she started to decline. Since Grampa had died, she hadn't had someone there to look after her. She had friends, but I could be there for her if she needed anything. And if I needed anything, she'd be there.

Suddenly, I was sure Mom must have set this up. I didn't know why she wouldn't tell us—maybe she didn't want either of us to think she was meddling—but it was the perfect solution. She could make sure someone was looking after her mom and her daughter at the same time. She'd never been crazy about the idea of me living somewhere that she wasn't sure would offer enough supervision.

Still, a little nagging sense of unease lingered after I hung up and went up to bed. It wasn't like my mother to be sly or sneaky. But what other explanation could there be?

Chapter Four

I crouched in the dark, a stone digging into my heel through the sole of my shoe. My heart raced in my chest, and I didn't dare breathe. Leaves rustled in the forest, and a stick cracked, followed by a tense, deliberate silence. Fear gripped me like a clawed hand, squeezing me until I thought I couldn't hold in a scream for one second longer. Just when I was about to make a sound, one of the shadows in the woods around me moved, a huge one detaching from the looming trees and creeping my way.

I choked back my scream. A pair of silvery moons shone out of the darkness at me. I couldn't see anything else, but I could smell the warm, wet animal scent of its pelt and a stink like rotting oranges on its breath. Sour bile spread over my tongue, and my legs went numb under me.

Just as I was about to collapse, a shadow slipped from beside me. Though it was still dark, I could see this one. A wolf stared unblinking at me, as still as a mountain and just as beautiful. Its fur was thick and blue-grey, its eyes a deep indigo like the ocean at twilight. I could fall into those eyes and disappear without a trace, a girl lost at sea. I could do nothing but stare back at the beautiful creature, as familiar to me as my own mind.

It seemed to know my mind, too. Those eyes knew not only my mind but my heart, my soul. It knew me as deeply and as surely as it knew the simple truth of the world, the mystery that wild animals knew but people could never unravel. No matter how many times it visited my dreams, I could never know its secrets the way it knew mine.

I stood transfixed, frozen in its spell as I always was, wanting nothing but to watch its massive form stand under the pines. But the shadow moved closer, looming over my wolf.

Fear ripped through my chest again as the shadow fell across the wolf. Instead of running, the wolf remained still, a sadness in its eyes like it knew. It knew what came next, and it accepted it in a way I never could. I opened my mouth, wanting to yell at the wolf to startle it so it would run away. Even if that meant I was left alone with the monster, I would have done it. But no sound came from my lips. I had been unable to stay quiet just a minute before, and now I tried to scream, but terror had frozen my tongue to the top of my mouth.

Before I could rip myself free of the paralyzing fear, the monster exploded into hundreds of shadowy wisps with tiny red specks of light for eyes. They dove onto the wolf, converging like angry wraiths, swarming until the majestic wolf was completely buried. Fear released its grip on me, and I opened my mouth and screamed.

I sat bolt upright, smothering my cry in my blanket, and yanked frantically at the chain on my lamp. Only when light spilled over the room did the shadows disappear. Light always drove away the monsters. Still, my breaths came short, and chills shuddered through me.

Only when I'd gotten up and turned on all the lights in my room did the cold begin to drain from my limbs. I still glanced into the corners ever few minutes, sure I'd see one of those sneaky shadows waiting to leap at me.

I pulled out my sketchbook and a charcoal-dusted bag of pencils. Setting them across my lap, I leaned back on my pillows and began to draw. I knew better than to go back to sleep. That would only make the nightmare return with more urgency. Drawing got them out of my head, onto the page. It made them real in a different way, a way that didn't make me seem completely crazy.

The next thing I knew, I heard soft footsteps and the flush of a toilet in my parents' bathroom. I yawned and stretched, setting my sketchbook aside and flexing my hand to work the cramping from my fingers. With a sigh, I threw off the blankets and went to my desk.

I opened my laptop and pulled up the website for Ravenwood again. Was I really going to let some creeped out feeling stop me from getting out of this town? I had lived with nightmares and monsters all my life. Whatever was already in my head was way creepier than my uneasy feeling about the academy.

Before I could second guess myself, I shot off an email thanking them and accepting their offer.

I sat back, a feeling of lightness in my chest for the first time in ages. I was about to close my laptop when I froze. My parents might be relieved to know I was somewhere that would force me to give up my all-black wardrobe and wear a skirt for once in my life, and my sister might be happy imagining I'd meet other weirdos like me at an artsy school. But Lindy... What would she do without me? What if she wasn't really a killer robot or spy? What if she was just a sad, quiet girl with no friends?

I grabbed a sheet of paper and dashed off a quick letter to her. I paused a minute, then pulled out another page from my notebook. This one took longer to compose.

Dear Alyvia, Amanda, and Makayla,

I'm sorry to say I'm leaving, and you'll no longer have the pleasure of pelting me with cruel words and jokes. Don't worry, I will fondly remember the year you turned all the girls against me. Oh, and when you got Danny to ask me out as a joke. Also the great times like when you laughed at me in the locker room, took a picture of my skirt tucked into the back of my underwear and sent it around school, or locked me in the supply closet.

I learned from the best.

That's right. All those years, I was taking notes in my Book of Evil, and you taught me well. Make no mistake. Even when I'm gone, I'll be watching you in my dreams. After all, I keep an eye on all the monsters of the world—including you. If you ever bother Lindy again, I'll see it, and I'll come back to make your life a hell darker than your worst nightmare.

Because in the end, you were right about me. I'm the real monster.

--T.

I thought I might have gone too far, but then I remembered that I hadn't worn a skirt in three years. My eyes still ached at the memory of having to walk down the hall while everyone laughed at my pathetic desperation in thinking a guy could want to go out with me. I decided that I owed Lindy at least this much. After all, with me gone, they'd probably pile all that on her. If I could do nothing else to protect her, at least I could do this.

I opened the mailbox and dropped the letter in. Just as I raised the flag, a dark cloud obscured the bright morning sun, and a shiver raced up my arms. Maybe my words had been a little too close to home. Because I had to admit, it wasn't just for Lindy. It had felt good to say the words I'd always wanted to say to those bitches.

Maybe I really was a monster.

Chapter Five

"Look," Josie said, grabbing my arm. I turned to peer out her rain-streaked window as the car wound along a narrow two-lane road through towering pines.

"Ravenwood Forest," I read, my heart stammering in my chest. I couldn't believe it. We were really doing this. Things like this just didn't happen to me. Not in a long time, anyway. I'd learned not to expect them.

"They have their own forest?" Josie asked.

"I'm sure it doesn't belong to the school," Mom said from the front. The wipers blurred back and forth on the windshield of our rental car, almost obscuring the view beyond the hill we'd just crested. A tiny, quaint town was nestled in the valley below. A shiver of anticipation worked its way through me, and I pulled my leather jacket tighter around myself, trying not to explode with anticipation. Gramma had moved to the nearest town a couple years before, but I'd never been here. She'd come to visit us every year, and once, Mom had gone up alone.

I turned back to the window, hiding my smile as Josie complained about how hungry she was after the long flight. I was too excited to be hungry. I flattened my hand against the window, watching the raindrops splatter against the glass. Outside, towering pines shadowed the road. Small bushes grew in the sandy, pine-needle laden ground under the trees. Suddenly, a sleek figure slid through the trees with a liquid grace I'd seen in my dreams. I jerked back with a gasp, then pushed forward, straining to see through the streaks of rain.

There's nothing there. Stop being such a freak.

I hugged myself even tighter, searching the woods for another glimpse of…Whatever I'd seen.

Which was nothing.

The car sped down the hill into the valley, leaving behind whatever figment of my imagination I'd conjured in the trees. "We on the right road, Timberlyn?" Dad asked from the driver's seat, interrupting my thoughts.

"GPS says yes," I said, waving my phone at him.

"Don't need a GPS with you in the car," he said. "You always know which way to go. You know what they say. A man never needs to stop and ask for direction… When he has a woman to tell him where to go." He laughed heartily at his own joke. "I say it's true if that woman is Timberlyn."

I rolled my eyes at my sister. It was true that I had a good sense of direction, but I couldn't exactly navigate roads I'd never heard of, let alone been on before.

"Your father's just teasing," Mom said. "Don't let it get to you."

"I'm not," I said, shaking my head at my sister.

"After we stop by your grandma's, we'll go visit this school that's so interested in you."

I ignored the hint of skepticism in his voice. He might not believe any school for the gifted was interested in his daughter—I barely believed it myself—but if they wanted me, I was sure as hell going.

A few minutes later, we pulled up at a little yellow house with white trim and multi-color pumpkins flanking the door, on which hung a wreathe of fall leaves.

"I didn't know Canadians celebrated Halloween," Josie said, hopping out of the car.

The sky was still spitting, and we hurried onto the covered porch together. "Let's see if they lock their doors," Dad said with a wink. "I always heard they didn't."

"Don't be silly," Mom said, knocking on the door. "My mother is not Canadian."

"She just moved here for the healthcare," Dad said, turning the knob.

Suddenly, chills exploded over my entire body. I whipped around toward the forest, sure I'd see... Something.

My heart lodged in my throat as Mom stepped inside. The terrible feeling had clamped around me like jaws, and I knew something terrible was about to happen. Or had already happened to Gramma. I turned and rushed into the house, brushing past Josie and Dad, sure I'd find Gramma sprawled out on the floor with a knife in her chest and her house trashed by intruders. Why else would her door be open?

"Is that you, Marla?" Gramma's high, hesitating voice called from another room. The scuff of shuffling footsteps approached, and Josie huffed about my rudeness for rushing in front of her. I tried to shake it off, laughing at myself for my jumpiness, but the unease lingered until I'd hugged Gramma and made sure she was as warm and breathing as the last time I'd seen her.

Dad went to get our bags, since we'd be staying for a few days, and Mom put on coffee. Gramma lifted the lid off a ceramic scarecrow and held it out to us. "Cookie?"

Josie and I took one to be polite, though I was still too spooked to do more than nibble at the edge.

"Everything looks better when you're eating a cookie, doesn't it?" she asked, her kind, watery eyes fixed on mine with such intensity I startled and nearly dropped my snack.

"Um, yeah," I said. "They're great."

"I knew it," she said, smiling and replacing the cookie jar. "They're always here if you need one."

"Thanks," I said, not sure what to say to that. I wouldn't be living here, and it wasn't like I'd be running over here every time I needed a cookie. Which, if Ravenwood was anything like PHS, would be daily.

But I wasn't going to think like that. Ravenwood would be different. It had to be. It was Canadian. Plus, it was a private school for art nerds, as far as I could tell. Surely I'd fit right in with them.

If you can keep them from seeing how crazy you are, a little voice inside me whispered.

I wandered to the back door and stood looking out at the rain and the woods. What if it hadn't been the other kids at my school who made me into a freak through some form of self-fulfilling prophecy? What if I'd always been one, and they'd sniffed out my difference the way kids could? They were more preceptive than adults, less prone to being fooled. Kid knew things, tapping into some kind of psychic, universal truth. Every Stephen King fan knew that.

"That's where they hide," Gramma said behind me.

I jumped and spun around, my hand squeezing reflexively and crumbling my cookie. "What?" I asked, my heart thudding again.

Rain tore at the screen in the window as if it could suck it into the forests and devour it.

"In the woods," Gramma said. "That's Ravenwood Forest. The town of Ravenwood is just over the mountain. That's where your school is."

"Did they run out of names?" Josie asked, scooting by Gramma with a fresh cookie in her hand.

"Oh, no," Gramma said. "It's all named after the town's founder. He was a prominent man in the area at one point. You can still visit Ravenwood Manor. He's gone now, though."

"What did you mean earlier?" I blurted. "You said something hides there. In the woods."

"I did?" Gramma asked, blinking at me with such confusion I started to wonder which of us was in worse shape. Was I hallucinating now?

"Never mind," I said, inhaling the cookie crumbs in my hand so I'd have something to distract me from the look Josie was giving me. It was one thing for Gramma to have a bad memory or say strange things on occasion. She was eighty. I was fifteen.

"Is the manor haunted?" Josie asked, her voice dropping dramatically as her eyes widened. "Does Mr. Ravenwood's ghost wander the forest, howling for his dead children... Who he murdered?"

I rolled my eyes and shoved my sister's shoulder playfully. "Cut it out."

"Hey, I thought you'd like that story," she said. "It's right up your alley. And you have to admit, those woods look all creepy in the rain. They're so dark."

She shuddered exaggeratedly, but I found a shiver creeping up my arms despite her dramatics.

"The Ravenwoods are long gone," Gramma said, ignoring our sisterly antics. "The most powerful local family is the Wolf family. In fact, Mr. Wolf's boys go to the academy, Timberlyn. I'm sure you'll meet them."

The hair on the back of my neck prickled, but I resisted looking out at the woods again. I'd already acted like a freak enough times in the past hour, and I knew that I'd see nothing if I looked into the woods, no matter how strong the sensation of being watched was.

"Are they cute?" Josie asked, giving Gramma a conspiratorial smile.

"Oh, yes," Gramma said, matching Josie's expression.

I watched with a mixture of longing and relief as Josie and Gramma cracked up. Not for the first time, I thanked the stars above that my sister and I weren't more alike. Sometimes, I wished someone understood the crap I had to go through, but I was glad my sister was so normal, despite having a freaky sister and Stepford parents. She would be just fine without me there. In fact, it removed the danger of her friends realizing that she might be tainted by her big sister's poisonous reputation.

With me gone, that would never happen. She'd get to grow up like a normal, happy kid.

"This rain doesn't look like it's going stop anytime soon," Mom said, appearing at the end of the hall with Dad close behind.

"We won't let a little rain stop us, will we, Timmie?" Dad asked, squeezing Mom's shoulder.

Before I could answer, Gramma's hand clamped around my arm with surprising strength, her thin fingers like skeletal claws as he nails dug into my flesh. "Stay out of the woods," she hissed, her eyes alight with fiery intensity.

"Okay, Gramma, chill," Josie said, scooting past her and heading for my parents. "No one's going in the creepy woods."

I glanced at my gramma again, coldness seeping into my veins where her hand clutched me. I gently detached myself, leaned in and pressed a kiss to her forehead. "I won't," I said, squeezing her hand before following my sister.

Dad was right. This was my chance to get out of my stifling little southern town, to move to a whole new country, to make the life I wanted for myself. Gramma's unhinged behavior and a little rain in the woods wasn't going to ruin that. I'd been given the rarest of opportunities, one most people like me never got, and I wasn't going to waste it. I'd been given the chance to start over, and nothing was going to stop me.

*

"Stop right there." The voice was so commanding that the four of us halted midstride, halfway to the door of the imposing building I'd seen in the photo online. The iron gates had allowed us in, but now a guy who must be a student strode toward us through the spitting rain, a scowl etched into his sculpted face. Despite his grim expression, he was unquestionably gorgeous, with shiny golden hair raked back from a high forehead, chiseled cheekbones, and wide, full lips that made my stomach flutter when I looked at them.

"We're here to enroll," Mom said, sounding nervous. I didn't blame her. Despite the guy looking young and wearing navy slacks, a white buttoned shirt, and a navy-and-red plaid tie that must be the school uniform, his enormous build gave him a commanding air.

"Who is?" he asked, his eyes moving over the group and locking on me. My heart did that stupid little flip again, but this time, it was accompanied by a rush of adrenaline. I knew a guy hopped up on his own importance when I saw one. I hadn't endured years of bullying without learning a thing or two about intimidation.

The guy's eyes widened, then narrowed, his nostrils flaring. "You must have the wrong school."

"Ravenwood, right?" Dad asked with forced, blustery cheer. "Our GPS got us here, so it must be the right school."

"I suggest your GPS take you elsewhere," the guy said, glaring at me like I'd personally shit all over his parade.

"Thanks," I said. "But unless you're in charge of admissions, you don't decide who's gifted enough to go here and who's not. I've already been accepted. Now, if you'll excuse us, I think we've stood in the rain long enough."

His hair and shoulders were now splattered with rain, but the rest of him was dry, making me wonder where he'd come from. He must have been sitting in a car somewhere, or he'd personally come out of another building to greet us. Either one was creepy, and I didn't appreciate his ordering me or my parents around.

Without waiting for him to reply, I headed for the tall, wooden front doors of the tan, brick building. It looked like it must have been around for a while judging by the towering turrets and spires of the roof. Dozens of tall, narrow windows showed from the face of the building, making it look like it would be light and sundrenched in better weather. It was definitely a far cry from the one-story prison-like cinderblock building I was used to.

Despite the odd encounter with the unfriendly guy, my heart picked up speed as we entered through the ten-foot wooden doors and stepped into a circular lobby with dark tile floors illuminated by a chandelier hanging from the vaulted ceiling as well as the numerous windows.

We headed for the office, where a nice woman pointed us to an office with ambient lighting and lush red carpeting. The nameplate next to the door said *Dr. Underwood, Headmaster*.

The administrator couldn't have been more different from the student I'd met. Dr. Underwood was a small, nervous-looking man in a bowtie with soft, cold hands and a weak handshake. Still, he smiled as he welcomed us and answered all our questions until we were all satisfied. I was more than satisfied. I'd almost forgotten the rude boy. No more small-minded Podunk High for me. I was going to a little artsy college-prep school where I could start over and be whoever I wanted to be. Maybe even myself.

By the time we'd finished talking to the headmaster, the rain had stopped. We walked along winding, curved trails to the dorm where I'd been assigned. We'd almost reached the building when a flash of movement in the woods caught the corner of my eye. I jerked around, sure

I'd see some looming beast or the sleek shape of an animal streaking between the trees.

"What's your deal?" Josie asked, looking at me like I was losing my marbles. Which apparently I was.

"Nothing," I said, shaking my head and hurrying ahead to put the building between me and the forest. We rang the doorbell, and the resident assistant let us in and pointed us upstairs to where we would find my room. As we climbed the stone steps in the old building, my heart began to pound. This was really happening. I was really moving here.

I stopped outside the door—209—and took a breath, wiping my hands on my black jeans before knocking. When I heard nothing from within, I inserted the key and pushed open the door. A tiny brunette with a pixie cut lay on one of the two twin beds, her shoulders propped against the wall and a book on her knees. Earbuds were crammed into her ears, which might excuse her failure to answer the door, but she barely glanced up at us.

"Hey, I'm Timberlyn," I said with a nervous laugh. "I guess I'm your new roommate."

"Delilah," she said, plucking one earbud from her ear.

"Did they tell you I was coming? I mean, we didn't bring all my stuff. I just wanted to say hi."

"Hey." With a disinterested shrug, she went back to her book.

Mom's dismayed expression left me scrambling for an excuse. The last thing I needed was for her to decide this wasn't the right fit. I could see the second thoughts piling up as my roommate continued to ignore us as we checked out the narrow bed and old-fashioned wooden desk on my side of the room. But I wasn't going back to PHS now. No way.

So maybe my roommate was a bit rude, but that didn't mean everyone would be that way. There were bitches everywhere, after all. It was unfortunate that I'd be living with one, but at least I could go to Gramma's on the weekends, and maybe I'd make some friends once I got to know people and found my place. No matter what, I wasn't giving up yet.

Even if it turned out this was just another small school with small minded people where I was a freak, so be it. I'd survive it. I'd been surviving for the last three years. And Gramma needed me here. I couldn't just give up and go back home, leaving her without anyone to look after her. I'd just have to stick it out and get used to Delilah. Maybe she was just shy and came across wrong. One thing was for sure. Despite the unpromising start, nothing at Ravenwood could be worse than what I'd already been through.

Chapter Six

A week later, I woke to my alarm. The grey sky outside spoke of rain, though for now, it seemed I'd be spared a downpour on my way to class. I sat up, swinging my legs off the side of the bed. A knot of nerves tangled in my stomach as I stumbled to the shower. When I returned, Delilah had disappeared. Apparently, my roommate would not be showing me around school on my first day.

Refusing to be discouraged, I pulled on the plaid skirt and white shirt the school had provided. Predictably, my parents had said it was an improvement over my all-black wardrobe, while my sister had laughed at me and asked if I was expecting a letter from Hogwarts. I smiled as I slid my arms into my leather jacket. My family had insisted on staying to help me get moved in, but they'd finally left. And even though they were a collective pain in the ass, I'd miss them.

I shook off the thought and picked up my backpack. No gloomy thoughts. New school, new me. Everyone in my entire family, from Josie to Gramma, would be better off.

I left my room and headed across campus, pulling my jacket closed as the damp, chill air tugged at me under the thick cover of clouds. I trotted up the steps to the main building. I'd been there during a school day, when everyone was in class, and on the weekend. Today, it was swarming with students. Plaid skirts blurred by, and for a second, a sickening wave of vertigo hit me, and I was nearly overwhelmed by all the matching uniforms, all the people I didn't fit with.

And then I realized that I looked just like them. For all they knew, I fit perfectly.

Clutching the straps of my bag, I took a step forward. Before I could dart through a gap in the milling uniforms, the most beautiful girl I'd ever seen slid from the crowd and floated over to me. She was nearly six feet tall, with the elegant grace of a dancer. Long, pitch black hair hung all the way to her elbows, and her alabaster skin was so flawless I had to fight not to reach out and touch it to see if she was real. Wide, violet eyes, delicate features, and a small, cupid's bow mouth completed her perfect face.

For one sickening moment, I was sure I'd made a horrible mistake. At least the mean girls at PHS looked like real people. If this genetically perfect girl was here to torment me, I might as well turn around and go home. Just looking at her was intimidating.

"You must be Timberlyn," she said, holding out a slender hand with long, fine fingers. "I'm Svana. I'm supposed to show you around, make sure you go to the right classes. All that." She gave a little laugh, sounding almost nervous, and suddenly, my fears melted. She wasn't here to call me an ugly duckling or ask if I was lost.

"Okay," I said as we started down the hall that had obviously been tacked onto the tall, round front entrance building at some point after construction. "I got my schedule already, and I looked at the map, so I think I'm pretty set. But if you wouldn't mind, maybe you can fill me in on some of the things Dr. Underwood left out."

Svana smiled, swinging her gorgeous hair back over her shoulder as we walked. "So, you're smart," she said. "That's good. You'll need it here."

"The classes are hard?" I asked. I wasn't surprised. The scant information on the website had told me as much. "Or the mean girls?"

"You know, I think you'll be just fine," Svana said. "You know the right questions to ask already."

I laughed at that. Apparently being a target for the past three years had been great preparation for boarding school. As I walked down the hall, though, I couldn't help but notice how freaking beautiful the people here were. Was it a boarding school or a modeling school? Svana was the most beautiful person I'd ever seen, and she wasn't the only one. Everyone seemed to be exceptionally gorgeous or at least striking.

"So, about those mean girls," I asked. "Want to point out a few people I should stay clear of? Unless you're one of them, and then I guess it's too late."

Svana laughed, a musical sound that frankly, made me a little jealous. Not that I sounded like a braying donkey or anything, but I didn't sound like an angel was inside me when I laughed, either. "Ravenwood's not really like that," she said. "I mean, yes, there are cliques for sure. Everyone here is exceptional, just in different ways. Some people are richer, or prettier, or more... Gifted. But the social situation is, like, each group keeps to itself. There are some conflicts between groups, but once you find your people, they'll have your back."

"It's more *West Side Story* than *Mean Girls*?" I asked.

Svana laughed again. "Something like that."

"And what if I don't find a group?" I asked. "Where do the loners hang out?"

Svana's pretty purple eyes widened, and she grabbed my arm and pulled me to one side of the hall, against a bank of lockers.

"What the—?" I started, but Svana made a shushing sound, cutting me off. Other people crowded against us, craning their necks to see down the hall. A hush fell over the hall, and the hair on the back of my neck prickled. Before I could ask again, a group of boys came striding down the hall. I immediately recognized the boy who had been so rude to us when I'd come with my parents. My heart did something completely inappropriate in response to his presence, as if it had come detached from my brain and decided to do its own thing. Which was dancing to the rhythm of his footsteps.

He led the pack, which moved with such synchronization it was as if they had one brain to share amongst the five of them. His muscles bulged against the jacket of his uniform, and I couldn't help but remember seeing those broad shoulders sprinkled with raindrops as his white shirt clung to his skin. I gulped and tore my eyes away, my heart hammering.

They didn't stroll, but moved slowly and deliberately, almost as if they were searching the rows of students lining the lockers for someone. Again, my heart did something funny, but this time it was a jolt of fear that gripped me. I had the absurd thought that he was looking for me.

A step behind the guy I'd met, walked two guys who were similarly gorgeous and similarly gigantic. On either side of them was one more guy, these ones just as massive but more light on their feet and lacking the family resemblance to the blond trio in the middle. Even though they looked nothing alike, they had the same aura as the blond guys, as if they shared some bond that transcended family and race.

As they drew closer, the girl beside us sucked in a breath. I turned to Svana to ask what the hell was going on. Her fingers dug into my arm, and she hissed, "Don't look."

I tried not to stare, though lots of other people were. Or...were they?

They seemed to be, but when the guys swung their heads in that direction, all eyes were lowered, gazes dropping to the floor. I glanced back at the guys, only to lock eyes with the rude one—the tallest, most thuggish looking of the five. His eyes were burning-cold, like frostbite. Despite the ice in his gaze, a hot shiver ran through my entire body, as if I'd been electrified from within.

Those eyes.

They were strangely familiar, a deep indigo blue. I was sure I'd seen them before, and not just outside the school that first day.

His lids lowered halfway, his nostrils flaring like he couldn't believe I'd dare to meet his eye. But I hadn't survived the last three years by scurrying away and hiding like a mouse. I held his gaze all the way down the hall even though my heartbeat was thundering in my ears and my palms were sweating.

The guys swept past without a word, and a collective exhale went down the hall. I joined it.

"What was that about?" I asked with an incredulous laugh.

"Those," Svana said slowly, "Are the Wolf boys."

"Ah," I said, feigning indifference. "My gramma mentioned them. Well, they seem lovely."

Svana laughed and stopped to point to a locker. While I did the combination, she explained. "Actually only three of them are the Wolf boys. The three white guys. Alarick is the leader. The rest of their posse is almost as bad, though."

"Good to know," I said. "You don't have to remind me twice to stay out of their way."

"Good," Svana said. "If you're smart, you'll stay far away. Basically, they appointed themselves as the unofficial gestapo of the school. If Alarick Wolf says jump, you better ask how high, or the other four will make you pay. They keep order—with their fists. And I hear their fists don't feel like butterflies."

"Headmaster Underwood definitely didn't mention that in the discipline policy," I said, pulling open my locker. Empty, of course. But full of so many possibilities. It seemed to symbolize my fresh start perfectly.

"Oh, don't worry about them," Svana said. "Just stay away from them, and you'll be fine. They don't go around bullying people. Just, if you get out of line…"

"They'll beat me up," I said. "Got it."

"I doubt they'd beat up a girl," Svana said. "Everyone's afraid of them, so people mostly do what they're supposed to. Even the headmaster is afraid of them."

"Seriously?" I asked, closing my locker after putting in my things. I gave the lock a spin and started toward my first class.

"Oh, yeah," Svana said, seeming all too happy to fill me in on the gossip as we walked. "Mr. Wolf, like, owns this town. Those boys have totally got Dr. Underwood in their pocket. And pretty much all the girls who go here."

I rolled my eyes at that. "Ugh, why?"

"Girls can't resist a bad boy," Svana said with a sly grin. "You know how it is. But they never keep the girls around for long."

"Which one are you in love with?" I asked, giving her a little nudge with my elbow so she'd know I was kidding. But I did want to know, just in case I started going on about how hot her guy was. I didn't want to piss off this girl who seemed to be my instant friend. I didn't know why. It seemed so incredible after PHS that anyone would even be friendly, let alone want to be my friend.

"None of them," Svana said. "I'm way too smart to think with my vagina."

"Okay then," I said with a laugh. I couldn't believe a girl I'd just met would say the word *vagina* to me. We definitely weren't in Arkansas anymore. Svana was so pretty she could obviously get away with saying anything, and she didn't seem to have much in the way of tact or fakeness. I appreciated that. Bluntness was a hundred times better than someone who would smile to my face and then stab me in the back the minute I turned to walk away.

As we approached the corner to the next hall, Svana said she had to get to her own class, but she'd catch up later. She made sure I knew where I was going and then with a wave, ducked into her classroom. I continued on, a real smile pulling at my lips. It was only my first day, and things were already a hundred times better here. Maybe I wasn't just like everyone else here, but no one could tell. There was a freedom in wearing a uniform. No one could judge me based on my clothes alone. And Svana hadn't treated me like a leper. Maybe everyone here would be as accepting.

My heart lightened as I hurried toward my class, a bounce in my step for the first time in years. As I turned the corner, I crashed directly into Alarick Wolf.

Chapter Seven

My collision with Alarick sent me stumbling backward, my binder and notebooks tumbling from my arms. The hall had emptied as a soft chime announced I was late to class. Perfect way to start my first day.

To my shock, Alarick bent and swept them all up into a disheveled pile between his giant paws. Only when he held them out to me did he seem to register who I was. He stood abruptly and shoved the stuff at me, a fierce frown darkening his brow. I moved automatically, taking the notebooks and clutching them to my chest as I stared up at him. God, he was huge. And frighteningly beautiful.

My heart thudded hard in my chest as the seconds ticked by.

Th-thump. Th-thump. Th-thump.

"I thought I told you to leave," he growled. His voice was deep and rough, a raw edge to it that made me think of someone who had been up all night screaming.

I shook off the weird effect he had on me. If I cowered to the bullies now, no matter how hot they were, I'd never survive the next four years. "I thought I told you I'd already been admitted," I said. "Maybe your dad forgot to cross out my name on the list of people you find unsuitable for your precious Ravenwood."

Alarick's eyes narrowed, and the hatred burning in those indigo eyes made me wince. It wasn't disgust and derision like the girls at home. This guy obviously despised me. I just didn't know why.

"You don't know anything about this place," he said slowly. "You don't know what you're getting into. If you did, you would have listened the other day."

"I'm not good at taking orders," I said. "Oops."

I shrugged and scooted away from the wall, edging past him. If I held the notebooks tightly enough, he might not see how hard I was shaking. If I held them in front of myself, it gave me a shield, no matter how ridiculously inadequate. It was more about the feeling of being shielded, being safer than if I had nothing between us, safer than having my heart exposed.

"If you're smart, you'll leave now and never come back," Alarick said. Before I could answer, he strode off down the hall, his footsteps hurried.

I stood watching him walk away, wanting to run after him for some ridiculous reason. I may not have been smart enough to heed his warning, but I was smart enough not to act on the impulse to stop him. Was I smart enough to follow Svana's lead and resist them, though?

Shaking myself out of my daze, I turned and hurried to class, my heart still skipping every few beats. What had he meant, anyway? Why was he so insistent that I not attend Ravenwood?

I walked in, so preoccupied I hadn't thought about the horror of walking into a freshman science class late as the new girl. I skidded to a stop next to the teacher's desk, every eye in the classroom fixed on me. Damn it.

"You must be Ms. Brink," said a balding, short man with a mustache. "Take an empty seat and follow along for today. Your table partner can fill you in on anything you've missed."

"Thanks," I mumbled, hating myself for being embarrassed. But this was a nightmare of similar proportion to finding a seat on the school bus when no one wanted to sit with you.

"Oh, and next time, please be on time, so you don't disturb the lesson."

Ouch. Well, I wasn't going to get any slack for being new at this school. I tucked my head down, held my books against my chest, and hurried to the only empty seat I saw at a glance. When I slid in, I relaxed for a second.

Until the guy beside me spoke. "I don't need a partner."

I looked up to find one of the Wolf brothers. I quickly scanned the rest of the class, thinking I could duck to another seat, but they were all full.

"Not my first choice, either," I said, flipping open my notebook. I had to get a grip on myself. I wasn't the shrinking violet type. My encounter in the hall had left me ruffled, that's all.

That was over, though, and now I had another one of these assholes to contend with. I had to put on my big girl panties and play tough whether I wanted to or not.

It wasn't so bad. I'd spent all day every day at PHS doing that. I just had to establish myself as someone not to be fucked with, and I'd be okay.

I expected the hulking blond to shove me out of my chair or something, but he didn't say anything. When I glanced at him from the corner of my eye, he was staring at me. He didn't look quite as hateful as his brother. In fact, the corner of his mouth was pulled up in a smirk. A small scar marked his chiseled chin, which showed the slightest hint of a dimple. He wasn't identical to Alarick. His nose was different, with a slight bump on the bridge, and his jaw was wider and squarer. But he had the same full but masculine lips as his brother, the same indigo eyes.

Damn, those eyes. They were so disconcertingly familiar, so beautiful but so eerie.

"See something you like?" he asked, adjusting the knees of his pants as he slouched down in his chair, drawing attention to his crotch. I could see a slight bulge through the navy fabric of the school uniform.

And now I was thinking about his penis.

I'd been warned to stay away from them, not think about them naked.

"Nope," I said, a beat too late. "Just trying to memorize the faces of the people I don't want to sit with tomorrow."

The guy smirked again and turned to face forward as the teacher gave an assignment to research a natural disaster. I groaned internally when he told us to work with a partner.

"I don't suppose you need a partner," I said, rolling my eyes at my desk mate.

"Nope," he said, sounding bored. "Lone wolf."

I could have pointed out that he actually traveled in a pack with his brothers and their friends, but I didn't want to poke the tiger, so I kept my mouth shut and raised my hand. "Can you assign me a group?" I asked when the teacher turned our way.

"Adolf, please work with Ms. Brink for today," the teacher said.

The blond scowled but angled his desk toward me.

"Your name is Adolf?" I asked. "Like, Hitler?"

"It means wolf," he said, his voice going deeper, almost a growl.

"So, your name is Wolf Wolf? Your parents must hate you. They might as well have named you Moon Moon."

Adolf's eyes narrowed, his fists clenching on his desk. "Don't talk about what you don't know, sweetheart. That pretty mouth of yours is going to get you in trouble."

"Your secret's safe with me," I said. I mimed a zipping motion across my lips.

LENA MAE HILL

Making fun of his name was probably not the best way to be invisible, but it had just popped out. How could I not say something?

"Do the project," he said.

"Okay," I said. "Which natural disaster should we do?"

Adolf pulled his phone from his pocket and thumbed it on. "I don't care," he said. "You wanted to be partners so bad, you do the work. Get us a B."

"Or what?" I asked. "You're going to get your daddy to call the school and complain so you can work alone again tomorrow?"

"Tell you what, Little Miss New Girl," he said, a smirk on his lips as his hand slowly inched up his inner thigh toward that bulge I'd been eyeing. "If you're so keen on getting near this, I'll take you out to my car right now and break you in. I do it with all the new girls who think they can handle it. It's kind of a tradition."

I didn't have an answer for that. The girls had been the worst at my old school, and needless to say, I had no sexual experience to speak of. I could only force myself not to react and start on the paper. But I was fuming inside. It would've been a lot easier to stay away from them if I didn't have to sit next to one of them.

Adolf made it really easy to want to stay far away, though. While I did the assignment, he sat there playing games on his phone. By the end of class, I couldn't wait to get out of there. I slapped the paper down on his desk in case he had to give final approval before turning it in, and then I marched out of class without a backwards glance.

I hoped his dad did call the school and complain, because there was no fucking way I could work with that guy again tomorrow.

I was just outside the door when a warm hand closed around my elbow. Startled, I looked up to find Adolf towering over me. Sitting down, it had been easy to overlook his size. Now he dwarfed my five-foot-five height by at least a foot, and he was so buff he probably could have tossed me over his shoulder and carried me around like a backpack all day if he wanted.

I noticed another girl glare death rays at me as she slipped past us, and she wasn't the only one who'd noticed the attention Adolf was giving me. Several pairs of girls stood whispering and staring behind Adolf, where he couldn't see them.

"What, did my work not measure up to your standards?" I asked, jerking my arm from his grip. The last thing I wanted was to make an enemy of these girls because of some attention that was definitely unwanted on my part.

"Watch what you say with that pretty mouth," Adolf said, leaning down to speak into my ear. I caught a whiff of his scent, a weirdly comforting smell that was a little like pine needles in a bonfire. He dropped his voice so low I could barely hear it. "My brothers wouldn't take it so well if you made fun of their names."

Without another word, he turned and slipped through the crowd, which parted like the Red Sea for his approach.

Well, shit. First I had to ponder why they didn't want me at Ravenwood so much, and now I was left wondering what Adolf's words meant. Did that mean he wasn't going to do anything, but that his brothers would if I said something similar to them? Or was he going to make my life hell because I wouldn't keep my mouth shut and worship him like everyone else did?

Not that I was immune. To my irritation, I felt shaky and a little jumpy as I started down the hall, and I had to stop and check my schedule because I'd forgotten my next class after the strange encounters with both the Wolf brothers. Not only that, but I could feel the eyes of the other students on me, separating me out. A dangerous pressure built behind my eyes, but I refused to let them see. Holding my head high, I began walking toward my class. I would get there. One step at a time. Deep breaths.

"Timberlyn!" A musical voice cut through the crowd, filling me with a ridiculous amount of relief. I felt my tension melting as Svana's willowy figure emerged from the pack of students, a boy in tow. He was even taller than her and just as thin and graceful, with the same jet-black hair and creamy white skin she had. He turned to watch Adolf's progression, a troubled expression on his gorgeous face.

"What was that about?" he asked quietly as we started down the hall.

"Your guess is as good as mine," I said.

"This is my brother, Viktor," Svana said, linking her arm through his. "Viktor, be polite."

"Sorry," Viktor said, turning forward from where he'd been glancing over his shoulder again. "Nice to meet you, Timberlyn. Welcome to Ravenwood. Didn't my sister warn you to stay away from the Wolf brothers and their thug posse?"

"Believe me, I don't need convincing," I said as we started down the hall again. "What's so bad about them, anyway?"

Viktor and Svana exchanged a look.

"My class is in the other wing," he said. "Svana just wanted me to meet you. I'll catch up with you at lunch. Just…stay away from them." He leaned in to give Svana a quick kiss on the cheek before slipping away into the crowd.

"Wow," I said. "Now I'm really intrigued."

"Don't be," Svana said with a shrug. "They're rich, entitled assholes who only care about themselves and get away with murder because their dad owns this town. Now, what do you have next? Art?"

That brought a smile to my face. I could only hope their art teacher was every bit as good as Dr. Underwood had made her sound. After all, that was the main reason I'd come here. After the morning I'd had, I just wanted to go in and lose myself in some sketches. I needed a distraction. Something to take my mind off the strange things the Wolf boys had said to me, the warnings flying at me from every side. I'd only made it through one class, and I was already wondering if I'd made a huge mistake.

Chapter Eight

I walked into my dorm room after school, dropped my bag, and fell face down on the bed. I wanted to groan, but Delilah was there, and I didn't want to give her more reasons to make the scoffing noise she made pretty much every time I said or did anything. I had spent the week at Gramma's, so this would be my first night in the room, and I wasn't looking forward to it. I sat up, suddenly wishing I had a mile walk home instead of just across the Ravenwood campus. After the day I'd had, I was more than ready to spend some time alone with my thoughts.

I glanced at Delilah, who was watching something on her laptop, her headphones over her ears, blocking me out entirely. But even if she ignored me, I knew she was there.

I rolled up and stepped into my closet, a walk-in with a light that made it a handy place to change out of my uniform without having to go to the bathroom down the hall. I pulled on a pair of yoga pants, a long-sleeve T, and a pair of tennis shoes. Grabbing my phone, I ducked out the door and left the dorm, heading for the woods.

The clouds still loomed overhead, somehow more foreboding because they hadn't delivered on their promise. I hesitated at the edge of the nicely manicured lawns of Ravenwood Academy. Beyond the school property, the woods looked almost as ominous as they had the day I'd arrived.

Get a grip, Timberlyn. The woods aren't going to eat you.

But just in case, I took out my phone and shot off a quick message to my sister. After all, even if the woods didn't eat me, and I didn't get attacked by monsters from my nightmares, I could always fall down a ravine or break an ankle on the unfamiliar terrain. After sending the text, I tucked my phone in the band of my pants and took off into the woods. Comforted with the knowledge that my sister would tell someone where I was if needed, my anxiety melted, and I took in the beauty of the forest.

After growing up in the south, where the forest could be downright jungle-like in summer, I found the towering pines stark but regal. The soft carpet of needles made my footsteps nearly silent as I walked, and there was very little underbrush to fight through, so I could keep up a good pace, exerting myself and clearing my head at the same time. The air felt fresh and crisp against my cheeks.

A soft snap in the woods behind me made me stumble. I spun around, my heart thudding in my ears now. Thunder rumbled across the sky, making a long, low rolling sound that raised chills on my arms despite having warmed up from the exercise. I scanned the woods. The steady sighing and singing of the wind through the trees, which had seemed lovely when I started out, now sounded more like wailing.

I tried to shake the thoughts from my mind. There was nothing in the forest behind me. The wind had snapped a small branch, making the sound that had startled me. The trees weren't wailing. I wasn't going to start acting as crazy as everyone back home had said I was. I was just taking a walk in the woods, and I was fine.

Just because people called me Timberloony didn't mean that I was nuts.

I turned and strode forward with more confidence, ignoring the shadows of the forest. To calm myself as I walked, I mentally ran over my day. On the plus side, I'd made an actual friend. Svana had grabbed me and insisted I sit with her and Viktor at lunch. He seemed a little slower to warm up and didn't share his sister's chatterbox quality, but he certainly hadn't been rude to me. Maybe in a few weeks, I could count him among my friends as well. Not only that, but my art class had turned out to be really cool and laid back. Ms. Stevens basically told me to pursue whatever medium I wanted and build a portfolio for her to grade at the end of the year.

On the minus side, I had classes with all three Wolf brothers, though it had been easy enough to avoid them after the two encounters that morning. If I could get out of partnering with Adolf again, I should be okay. Alarick hadn't hunted me down to demand why I was still there later in the day, so maybe he'd accepted that I wasn't going to leave just because he wanted me to. Adolf had passed me in the hall later and completely ignored me since he had a handful of other girls fluttering around him like butterflies. The third brother hadn't even looked at me, and none of the girls in school had made fun of my clothes, called me crazy, or left nasty surprises in my locker.

A bird screeched somewhere above, and I looked up, trying to spot it through the tossing trees. The sky had darkened even more as evening came on, and another rumble of thunder echoed across the sky. Suddenly, the hairs on the back of my neck prickled, and shiver gripped my body as a cold certainty filled me. I was not alone.

My heart hammering, I turned slowly, a fist of fear locking in my throat.

Just ahead, through the trees where I'd been aiming, stood a giant wolf.

I stumbled backwards, my legs turning to liquid. I nearly screamed when my back touched something, though my fingers told my brain it was just a tree. I gripped the rough sections of bark, trying to swallow the fear that threatened to overtake me.

The wolf stalked forward, its head lowered slightly, dark eyes locked on mine. My entire body began to shake uncontrollably as it came closer, emerging from between the trees. Even my brain seemed to be shutting down, so that my thoughts came from outside myself.

I'm going to die. It's good that I texted Josie, though. At least my parents will know what happened.

The animal was enormous, bigger than I'd ever imagined a wolf… Except the ones in my dreams. Was I dreaming? Had I fallen asleep on my bed when I flopped down on it, and this was a dream? It had to be a dream. But it felt so real.

I could see the wolf's thick pelt rippling in the wind that gusted through the trees, could see the stiff hairs on its ruff bristling as it stalked me like prey. I could hear the low rumble in its throat as it drew nearer. I could smell the promise of rain in the damp air, the dry pine needles beneath my feet and the living ones in the trees overhead.

And then a fat drop of rain hit my cheek. The cold of it, the wetness, shocked me back into myself. This was no dream.

I eased my body sideways, glancing into the trees ahead. The wolf snarled, the skin on its muzzle wrinkling as it bared long, sharp fangs.

Oh, shit.

Any thought of moving slowly fled. I turned to run, my heel slipping on a loose rock. I fell halfway, catching myself with my hand. The pain that shot up my arm when a sharp pebble cut into my palm only confirmed that this time, my nightmare was real.

I scrambled to my feet, sure that at any second, those deadly fangs would rip into my leg, crippling me so I couldn't escape. Without looking back, I ran.

Pine needles shifted under my feet, but they were surprisingly solid. The lack of underbrush let me fly back toward Ravenwood at a pace I wouldn't have believed. I wasn't a runner. I liked walking, but I was usually leisurely about it, savoring every minute of solitude. No one would have guessed today. I sprinted through the woods like the devil himself was on my heels.

Maybe he was.

I tore through the woods, outrunning everything but the rain, guided by nothing but instinctual fear. By the time I arrived back at the dorm, I was drenched all the way through, but I'd halfway convinced myself that I'd imagined that. There was no way I'd seen an oversized, blue-eyed wolf in the woods. There was no way I'd run from it, and it hadn't chased me. I must have let my fear get the best of me, imagining things like I had the day I arrived in Ravenwood. Nothing but groundless fear had been behind me, like a child running from the dark.

When I pushed open the door to my room, out of breath and dripping wet, my roommate glanced up from her laptop. Her eyes narrowed as I dropped my wet phone on the nightstand with a clatter. She yanked out one earbud and glared at me.

"Where have you been?" she asked, her voice deliberate and almost accusatory.

"Out," I said, twisting my long red hair up and securing it with an elastic.

Delilah shook her head and put her earbud back in. "Whatever," she muttered as I stepped into my closet to change into dry clothes. I peeled my shirt over my head, then my sports bra. My skin prickled with chill, and again, I pictured that wolf. A wolf that stood almost as high as my shoulders, with silvery grey fur and eyes the color of the ocean at twilight.

I paused with a dry shirt clutched in my hands, my heart hammering all over again.

Those eyes.

Eyes the exact shade of indigo as the eyes of the Wolf brothers.

Chapter Nine

That night, I slept fitfully. Dreams of wolves and boys with indigo eyes battled for space in my nightmares. I woke each time, scolding myself for making the association between the weird sighting in the woods and the boys' last name. Around dawn, I gave up and slipped out of bed to draw by the scant light creeping in the window.

Luckily, my phone had dried out, and I was able to retrieve the two-word text my sister had sent late the night before.

You alive?

I smiled and sent her a message to assure her I had made it back. In the pale light of morning, the day before seemed more like a dream than ever. I decided not to think too hard about it and start driving myself crazy— and not to go back into the woods. If I was losing my mind, I didn't want to know quite yet. As soon as I saw other students starting to emerge from their dorms, I headed out through the foggy morning for my second day at Ravenwood.

When I walked in the front doors of the school, I was instantly aware of a quiet buzz of conversation that hadn't been there the day before. I glanced around, a moment of paranoia gripping me. But no one was looking at the new girl. Groups of students huddled together, talking in hushed voices. A few gave me curious looks when I walked by, but nothing more than they'd give any other unfamiliar face.

The charge in the air made me hurry my footsteps, though, wondering what had happened. Had someone else seen the wolf in the woods? A mixture of dread and excitement filled me when I caught sight of Svana and

Viktor leaning on the wall. I was sure that whatever happened, Svana would know about it.

"What's going on?" I asked, joining the two of them. For one long, tremulous moment, I thought she was going to tell me to go away, mind my own business. That yesterday she'd been nice because it was my first day, but that we weren't friends. I realized that today was even more important than my first day at Ravenwood. Today, I would either build on our new friendship or be left to fend for myself. Everything hung on the one moment between my question and her answer.

Svana's eyes widened, and she leaned in, keeping her voice low. "You didn't hear?"

"No," I said, matching her voice with mine. "What happened?"

There was another second where everything hung in the balance. A moment when I'd become something more than the crazy girl whose only friends were the monsters in her notebook. For the first time in years, I had a friend. Someone who wanted to share gossip with me instead of spreading gossip about me.

And then she answered.

"Brooklyn is missing," she said. "She never came back from dinner last night. Her roommate thought maybe she'd snuck out without telling her, and she'd come home late. But she hasn't shown up this morning."

I remembered that name from my science class the day before. I hadn't spoken to the girl, but she'd given me death glares when she walked out of class and saw me talking to Adolf. Suddenly, I wished more than anything that she'd now come walking in and make some rude comment to me, the way I'd been afraid she would. But somehow, I knew it wouldn't happen. There was a strain of shock and certainty in the air. Something was wrong.

My skin went cold, and I wrapped my arms around myself, grateful for the leather jacket I'd worn again today. "It's only eight in the morning," I said. "Maybe she partied too hard, and she's sleeping off a hangover."

"Maybe," Svana said. "But that's not likely."

"But it could be true?" I pressed.

"This is a small school, Timberlyn," Viktor said, frowning down the hall. "Almost everyone at Ravenwood came from the mainland, so it's not like we're going to know people in town who don't go to this school."

"If we go out and party, we go with other people from the academy," Svana said. "And if there's a party, everyone knows about it, and it's not on a Monday."

"Yeah," I said. "I was just hoping…"

Viktor's breathtaking lavender eyes focused on me, and his expression softened. "I know," he said. "We're all hoping. But that's not what happened."

I wanted to ask how he knew, but I held my tongue. Everyone was on edge. I could tell as I went about my morning classes. A hushed numbness seemed to grip half the student body, making the walk between classes feel like a funeral march. I got more curious glances today, when things were quiet and subdued. People were looking for anything astray, anything that didn't fit the norm.

By lunch time, I was anxious to know if there had been any new developments. At PHS, I'd always eaten in the art room. I had a sneaking suspicion my art teacher had taken pity on me because she'd been an outcast in her own past. But here, I didn't have to hide at lunch. Svana had sought me out the day before, going through the food line with me and chatting the whole time, then leading me to a table as if she'd just assumed that I would know I had a place with her.

It had been a long time since I had a place with anyone, and I nearly teared up with gratitude when I walked into the dining room and saw Svana waving me over. "Sorry, we got out of fourth period early," she said, motioning at her plate. "But Viktor's saving you a spot in line."

She hadn't started eating, so I hurried to find her brother so we wouldn't keep her waiting too long.

"There you are," he said, motioning for me to join him in line. I hesitated, not wanting to cut the line. A couple people glanced at us, but they looked less angry and more like they were trying to figure out whether there was something going on with me and Viktor. I stepped into line but left a little distance between us, not wanting to step on any toes like I had with Brooklyn. Viktor was unearthly beautiful, so there was no way that he wasn't lusted after by half the girls in school. The half that liked quiet, broody guys instead of bulging muscles and intimidation.

"Any news on Brooklyn?" I asked, keeping my voice low. Still, the two girls in front of me fell silent.

Viktor shifted and stuffed his hands in his pockets. "We would have heard if she was back," he said.

"Are the cops investigating yet?" I asked. "Or do you have to wait twenty-four hours or something?"

"I don't know," Viktor said, shuffling forward to the food. He took a plate and handed me one. The food at Ravenwood was a far cry from American public school cafeteria fare, with meat that was actually identifiable as a real part of an animal and seasonal vegetables that had never seen the inside of a can. I took a chicken leg and some maple-glazed butternut squash. Viktor took the same, not seeming to notice what he was getting. He grabbed two glasses and passed me one. We filled our cups at the soda machine and headed for Svana's table. To my surprise, Delilah was sitting across from her, leaning forward and speaking with animated gestures.

"Y'all know my roommate?" I asked Viktor as we made our way to the small oak table. The dining room held only about fourth of the school at once, Dr. Underwood had explained, so there were four lunch periods. Instead of splitting the student body by grade, as PHS had, lunch time was organized around our schedules. The dining room was large, with an assortment of vintage wooden tables spread through the room instead of crammed together.

"Everyone knows each other at Ravenwood," Viktor said in answer.

Delilah finished whatever she was saying to Svana and rose just as we arrived. "I'm late to class," she said, pushing back and standing from her chair. "See you guys later."

She waved, and for the first time since I'd met her, she smiled. It was all for Viktor, though. She barely glanced my way before turning on her heel and disappearing out the doors.

"Girlfriend?" I asked Viktor, taking the seat she'd vacated.

"No," he said, scooting my chair in for me and taking the seat beside me. Svana had pushed her plate aside, and I felt guilty that she'd waited. Her chicken would be cold by now. But she said she needed a refill on her drink and left the table.

"Sooo," I said, digging into my lunch. "Did I hit on a nerve? You and Delilah used to date?"

At first, I thought Viktor was going to tell me to mind my own business. He poked at his chicken, then made a face and nudged his plate aside, picking up his soda instead. "A couple times," he said at last, shooting me a sideways glance. "It wasn't serious, though. Nothing happened."

I didn't want to dissect what that might mean. Nothing sexual?

I swallowed at the thought, still too inexperienced to be anything but awkward with that topic of conversation. "Any idea why she hates my guts?" I asked, trying to sound light.

"She's been here a few years," Viktor said. "Longer than a lot of us. She's probably just intimidated by new girls. Once you've been here a while, someone else will come along to threaten her."

"Threaten her?" I asked, pausing mid-chew. "How am I a threat?"

Viktor shrugged, turning his glass on the table. "I don't know," he mumbled. "You're new. You're getting attention. You're pretty. You could replace her."

There was so much in those short sentences that I could analyze. Viktor the Gorgeous thought I was pretty. That my roommate might be threatened by me somehow taking her place as an attention grabber instead of thinking I was a crazy freak. I had noticed a few curious gazes throughout the day, but I hadn't really thought of it as attention. I certainly hadn't done anything to attract it. The most daring thing I'd done had been to make friends with some of the more gorgeous people at the school.

Well, that wasn't exactly true. I'd mouthed off to the Wolf brothers.

I looked up at that thought, my eyes automatically drawn to the table where they'd sat the day before. The three of them, along with their two esteemed lackeys, sat at a round table next to the huge windows and the door. And all five of them were staring at me.

Before I could tell my heart the appropriate response, it flip-flopped in my chest then took off at a dead sprint. I had to grab my soda and swallow a big mouthful to avoid choking on my food. Why were they staring at me like that?

"What's their problem?" I asked, ducking my head and speaking sideways to Viktor.

"Who?" he asked, looking up when I nodded my head in the direction of the Wolf brothers. When I looked up, though, they were all eating and talking as if nothing had happened. As if they hadn't just been staring at me with three identical pairs of ocean-at-twilight eyes.

Those damn eyes. Those eyes that had haunted my dreams, haunted my walk yesterday. Was I cracking up, losing my mind? Viktor was looking at me in confusion, having not seen anything but the five goons eating and goofing off the way everyone else in the dining room was doing. Had I seen that? Or was I imagining that, too?

"Nothing," I muttered as Svana joined us again.

"So," she said, taking a sip of her soda and adopting a teasing tone. "Your roommate says you were out late last night."

"What?" I asked. "No, I wasn't. I mean, I went out for a walk after school, but I wasn't out late. I came back before dark."

"Where'd you go?" Svana asked.

"Nowhere," I said, feeling suddenly and inexplicably defensive, though her tone was friendly.

"O-kay," she said, giving me a funny look.

After a moment of awkward silence, I shoved a bite of chicken in my mouth. "You're not eating?" I asked.

"I live on Diet Coke," she said, taking another swig.

I felt like a pig downing my food, but I wasn't really the dieting type, so I finished my food anyway. We moved on from Delilah to safer topics, including our homerooms and the emergence of the sun at last. As we walked out of the dining room, Svana waved and headed out toward her next class, which was in a building off the side of the small one that housed the kitchen, dining room, and common area.

Just as Viktor and I stood, I felt the prickle on the back of my neck that was beginning to feel too familiar. I turned to find the Wolf brothers approaching, a scowl on Alarick's face. My eyes met his indigo ones, so like my dream, so like...

The wolf.

It hadn't been a dream.

"Can I walk you to class?" Viktor asked.

"Uh, sure," I said, though I wasn't sure what had just happened.

"Let's go before they see you staring," Viktor said, looping his arm through mine and hurrying us outside.

"Wow, you really don't like them, do you?" I asked.

"Sorry," Viktor said, quickly dropping my arm.

"It's okay," I said.

"Sorry if I seemed unfriendly at lunch," Viktor said, falling into step beside me.

"You didn't," I said. I wasn't about to lose my chance at having friends by being too bitchy. It was one thing to act that way to my tormentors, and though it was easy to fall back on that because it had been my main form of communication over the past few years, Viktor and Svana had been ninety percent awesome since I'd arrived.

"I guess I'm a little shy," Viktor said, not meeting my eyes. "Sometimes that comes across as dickishness. Or so I've been told."

I couldn't help but laugh. "Not at all. You don't owe me anything. You don't know anything about me. There's no reason for you to be nice to me."

Viktor peered at me from the corner of his eye. "That's… And odd thing to say."

"It is?"

"Why wouldn't I be nice to you? When you're the new kid, everyone should go out of their way to be nice to you. How else do you know where you'll fit in?"

"I hadn't thought of it like that," I admitted. I'd been so busy worrying about a repeat of PHS that it hadn't occurred to me that people would be nicer to me simply because I was new. In truth, no one but him and Svana had been especially welcoming.

"Don't worry," Viktor said. "When everyone else works up the nerve to talk to you, you'll find your place."

"What if my place is with you?" I asked. I immediately winced at the words. They sounded so flirty, so forward. I didn't even know if I wanted to flirt with Viktor. He was undeniably, unnaturally gorgeous, but my heart hadn't skipped a beat when he took my arm. All I had to do was think about Alarick, and my pulse started racing.

Shit. What was I doing? Viktor was nice, and maybe, possibly, if I ever dated someone, he could be an option if he liked me. The Wolf brothers? No.

A short, awkward silence had met my question, but at last Viktor cleared his throat. "I'm sure you'll have a lot of options," he said. "We don't have a lot of friends, as you can tell. We're pretty new here, too. We have a little circle, though."

"You're new, too?" I asked.

"We've been here a year," Viktor said.

"Cool," I said, grateful to have a safe, easy topic of conversation. "Where'd you move from?"

"Iceland."

"Wow," I said, letting out a little laugh. "I thought I'd come from a long way. Did you come just for Ravenwood?"

"Yes," he said. "We were lucky to both be accepted."

"You barely have an accent," I said. "I can't believe you've only been here a year."

"It helps to make friends when you know everyone here has come from all over the world. A lot of us feel like out of place or like the new kid."

"Thank you," I said, that teary feeling of gratitude warming me again. I couldn't believe he was being so nice to me, and for no other reason than he wanted to help me feel welcome. "That does help. A lot."

"I'm glad," Viktor said, offering me a small, closed lip smile that made him even more adorable if that was possible. "If you have any questions about Ravenwood, I'll do my best to answer them."

"Maybe a few," I admitted, thinking of those boys whose eyes had haunted my dreams before I met them. This wasn't in itself an anomaly. I'd dreamed about people on occasion. But dreaming of a person and then meeting them… The one time that had happened, it had led to my three-year fascination with Lindy back home. If my physiological response to the boys was an indication, I was working on a new obsession.

"Tell me about the Wolf brothers," I said at last, deciding on the straightforward approach.

Viktor frowned, obviously not happy with my choice of questions. But he hadn't put a stipulation on the offer to answer questions, and I intended to find out all I could from anyone who would talk to me. I'd never solved the mystery of why I'd dreamed of Lindy. This time, I'd figure it out.

"What do you want to know?" Viktor asked. "I thought my sister told you."

"What about their family?" I asked. "She said they own the town. Do they literally own property around here?"

I tried to sound casual, but my pulse thundered in my ears as I waited for his answer.

"A lot," he said. "Mr. Wolf bought up just about everything in the valley that wasn't privately owned."

"What about the forest behind the school?"

"Yeah, I think so," he said, giving me some side eye. "Why? Timberlyn, did you see something?"

I could barely swallow, and I regretted eating that delicious lunch. I should have just sipped a soda like Svana. "What do you mean?" I asked, though my voice came out as not much more than a whisper. "What would I see?"

"If you saw something, you have to tell someone," Viktor said. "If you saw Brooklyn going into the woods, or… Or those guys…" He broke off and shook his head.

Brooklyn. Shit. I hadn't even been thinking about her. Suddenly, my stomach clenched with a new kind of fear, and cold gripped me. "You can't think they'd actually kill someone," I whispered.

I remembered that wolf in the woods, its eyes fixed on me so intently, the size of those teeth. I began to tremble all over just remembering.

"I'm sorry," Viktor said, putting an arm around me. "I didn't mean to scare you. It's just… When I told you to stay away from them, I meant it. They're dangerous. If someone crossed them, and they were pissed… You should tell Dr. Underwood if you saw Brooklyn last night."

"I didn't," I said, ducking out from under his arm.

"Okay," Viktor said, but he didn't sound convinced. At all.

"Just forget I asked," I said.

"Timberlyn," he said. "I didn't mean to be an ass. I just wanted to warn you. Stay out of their way. Guys like that think the rules don't apply to them. They think they can get away with anything—because they do."

As we reached our classroom, that eerie silence fell in the hall, and my skin prickled, and I knew who was walking behind us. My heart tripped over itself, and it wasn't just fear. There was something else, something stupid and reckless and the opposite of self-preservation.

I turned to watch them, captivated by the way they walked together as one, like they were all part of the same being. They didn't strut or stroll lazily, lording their power over everyone else. And yet, everyone fell back to let them walk by, like a slow-motion scene in a movie with a badass soundtrack.

As they walked by, all five heads swiveled our way, and a chill exploded across my skin, racing from the crown of my head to the tips of my toes. I bit my lips together to keep from gasping out loud when five pairs of identical, indigo eyes locked on me. But I didn't drop my gaze and shuffle away like everyone else. Instead, when they kept staring, I met Alarick's eyes and bugged out my own eyes at him to let him know how obvious he was being.

When they passed, their heads swiveled to look back at me over their shoulders for another second. Then they swung around to face forward and continued on, and the weird slo-mo trance that had fallen over me snapped. For a second—or had it been longer?—it had been as if no one existed but the six of us. Something had passed between us, some promise that I didn't understand. And I didn't think it was a promise of anything good to come. I felt like I'd just been marked, painted with a target on my forehead. Cold dread settled in my stomach, and I stumbled back against Viktor, suddenly aware that everyone in the entire hallway was staring.

"What are you doing?" Viktor hissed. "I just told you not to draw their attention."

"Sorry," I muttered. "I don't like bullies. I don't like people thinking they have power over other people. No one's better than anyone else. Someone needs to stand up to them."

"True," Viktor said. "But it doesn't need to be us."

Maybe not, but I had a feeling it was going to be us. I didn't think I was going to have a choice in the matter. If they were going to make my life hell, I was glad I had at least a couple friends to have my back. I was going to need them. Because I'd vowed when I came to this school that things would be different. If someone fucked with me, they better be ready for a fight. Because I wasn't going to roll over and die. The Wolf boys might think they ran this school, and I'd bow down to them and follow their rules, but they had a surprise in store.

They'd might have been ruling Ravenwood until now, but they'd just met their match. Because I was just crazy enough to question their rule.

Chapter Ten

The next day, there was still no word on Brooklyn. Finally, during the last period of the day, they filed us all into an old, beautiful auditorium. With lights running along the red-carpeted aisles, red velvet curtains on a real stage, padded wooden seats, and a balcony with additional seating, it couldn't have looked further from the ancient gym PHS had used for assemblies.

I craned my neck, looking for Viktor and Svana. It hit me again that I had friends. I had people to look for instead of just scuttling to the top row in the back corner where I could pretend to be bored while really keeping an eye out for incoming spitballs. Here, I had people to seek out, just like everyone else. Here, someone was waving to me and calling my name, beckoning me. I floated toward Svana, trying to keep the silly grin off my face. A sense of wonder set in. Someone actually sought my company. I wasn't just looking for someone. Someone was looking for me.

I hurried over and slid into the seat she'd saved for me, feeling like I'd just won the lottery instead of an upholstered red seat. No one had ever saved a seat for me before.

And then I felt the prickle on my neck, and a rush of goosebumps swept over my skin. I turned to see Donovan, the third Wolf brother and the only one who hadn't talked to me, standing in the aisle next to the row behind us. My eyes were nearly level with his belt buckle, and I couldn't keep my eyes from dropping, or the heat that crept to my cheeks when I realized I was eyeing his package. I blamed the uniforms. They made the temptation somehow irresistible.

"Move," Donovan said, his voice hard and flat.

My heart skipped, and I glanced around, about to stand before I realized he was talking to the people behind us. They were scrambling to get out of his way, abandoning their seats like rats leaping from a sinking ship. "What is he doing?" I asked, grabbing Svana's arm.

"They always choose where to sit," she said. "It's part of their reign of terror. At least they didn't pick our row."

"No," I muttered, my heart racing. "Just right behind us."

Delilah, one of the displaced students, gave Donovan a death stare as she filed from her seat. But when she reached him, and he stared her down from a foot and a half higher than her, she dropped her eyes and stomped off. I decided to try again with her. Maybe she needed a friend now, too.

Alarick arrived beside his brother and muttered, "What the hell, dude?"

"You told me to choose," Donovan said.

"Not here," Alarick said, sounding beyond annoyed. "Anywhere but fucking here."

I couldn't help but wonder what was the big deal about here? Was it me? Was Alarick actually trying to avoid me? He definitely hadn't gone out of his way to talk to me since my first day. He'd stared at me a few times, but that was it. Adolf had made a few rude comments, but mostly he was just lazy in science class. Donovan was in my art class, but he sat in the back corner and never talked as far as I could tell. The other two guys in their gang, Vance and Jose, hadn't paid me any attention beyond staring, either.

After a couple more muttered curses, the boys must have agreed this was acceptable, because they all sat, the tiny seats groaning under their massive weight. My whole body felt charged just knowing they were all there. I swear I could almost smell the overwhelming masculinity of them, all those muscles and hormones raging behind me. My skin was tingling with heat, and I kept having to shift in my chair, my breathing shallow and my limbs tensed for... Something.

Before anything more happened, Dr. Underwood scurried out on stage. The bright lights on the stage reflected off his bald head as he adjusted the mic and cleared his throat. "I'm sorry to announce we are here for a sobering reason this afternoon," he said after a minute of preliminary shushing and a reminder of his position. "As I'm sure you are all aware, we had a student go missing on Monday night. We still have no information regarding the whereabouts of the student, but we are working with law enforcement to bring her back safely to the Ravenwood family."

A low snort of derision sounded behind us. I glanced over my shoulder. Donovan's hands were clutched around the arms of his seat, his eyes so dark they appeared black in the dimmed lighting.

Viktor gave him a dark look from where he sat on Svana's other side.

"If you have any information you think would be helpful to the investigation, if you spoke with Brooklyn in the past few days before her disappearance, if she said anything strange, please come by the office and let one of us know. We've also set up an anonymous tip line for anyone who might feel anxious about involving yourself."

He went on about how they had no reason to believe anything bad had happened, but that we couldn't be too careful. I tried to pay attention, but I'd never been more aware of my body. It seemed to be screaming for every bit of my attention. I was painfully aware of it and of everything around it. Finally, Dr. Underwood concluded with a warning.

"Until Brooklyn returns, the safety of every student is our top priority. At this time, we do ask that you use extra caution when moving around campus. Please walk with a friend between buildings, especially in the evening or when other students are not around. And most importantly, remember that you are required to check out through the administration when leaving campus, even if you're going to visit parents or friends in town and plan to be back in a few hours."

With that, they dismissed us. Everyone began to group up, murmuring and casting glances around. The administrations' calming words had done nothing to reassure us. I didn't stand or even look back, but I could feel the presence of the boys looming behind me as if the monsters from my dreams were closing in. I gripped the arms of my chair and closed my eyes.

"Timberlyn Brink?" said a firm female voice. My eyes snapped open, and I found myself looking up at a woman I recognized as the dean of students.

"Y-yes?" I asked, straightening in my chair. I expected the Wolf brothers to hurry off in the presence of an administrator, but they were just standing over us, watching. Suddenly, I remembered Svana's words. They ran the school. They could do whatever they wanted. What if Alarick had decided that if I wouldn't heed his warning, he'd have the school expel me?

But for what?

"Can we see you in the office?" Dr. Rowe said, her mouth set in a grim line.

I cast a glance at Svana and Viktor, whose faces reflected my own confused expression. I stood and followed Dr. Rowe, but not without narrowing my eyes at Alarick to let him know that I wasn't stupid. I knew who was behind this, whatever it was. I'd had plenty of time in my life to fantasize about having laser eyes to shoot people, and I gave him my best death glare as I followed Dr. Rowe in what suddenly felt like a death march. Students fell silent, their eyes turning my way as we passed.

In the office, Dr. Underwood sat at his round table. He told me to take a seat, and I obeyed while Dr. Rowe took another chair. "You're not in any trouble right now," Dr. Underwood assured me. "But you understand we have to treat this matter very seriously. We can't leave any suspicious activity unexamined."

Suspicious activity?

"Okay…" I said, knotting my hands together in my lap.

"It was brought to our attention that you left campus on Monday night," Dr. Rowe said. "The night Brooklyn was last seen on campus."

Wow. What the actual fuck? I couldn't believe I'd just been thinking about trying to make friends with my roommate.

"Can you tell us your whereabouts that day, between when you left your room and when you went to dinner?" Dr. Rowe asked.

"I went hiking," I said through gritted teeth. "Is that a crime?"

"No," Dr. Rowe said. "But as you know, you're required to get a pass to leave campus. Did you leave campus, Ms. Brink?"

"Yes," I admitted after a pause. There was no use in lying now. "I guess I forgot about that rule. I was just going for a walk. I didn't know I had to check out for that."

"You left campus," Dr. Rowe said.

"I only hiked in the woods," I said. "I didn't see Brooklyn or anyone else."

Unless you count freakishly large wolves with eyes that somehow match those of your thugs.

Dr. Rowe was looking at me like she obviously didn't believe a word coming out of my mouth. The look on her face said it all. I was a bad kid, one who didn't follow the rules and sign out before setting foot off campus. She'd already decided, and no matter what I said, she wasn't going to change her mind.

"Where exactly did you go?" Dr. Underwood asked, licking his lips and glancing at the dean.

"I don't know," I said. "I walked behind the dorm, in pretty much a straight line."

"Those woods are private property," Dr. Rowe said. "There are signs posted all along the edge of the trees. Didn't you see them? Or did you *forget* those, too?"

"We have a fully equipped gym with treadmills and weight equipment," Dr. Underwood said. "You can always exercise there. We just don't want any students putting themselves or anyone else in danger."

I took a deep breath to calm my rage. "Look, I get it. You're freaked out because a student disappeared, but I didn't, and I had nothing to do with her. I barely know who she is. I made one stupid error in judgment, and I'd appreciate it if you didn't make me feel like a suspect just for taking a hike. Next time, I'll check out. Now, are we done here, or do I need a lawyer?"

They exchanged a look that only made my ragey-ness increase.

"We're done," Dr. Rowe said.

"Make sure you walk home with a friend," Dr. Underwood called as I headed for the door, still fuming.

"That would be a lot easier if you hadn't held me until everyone else was gone," I muttered as I stepped into the hall. The door clicked closed behind me, the sound echoing in the huge, round chamber that formed the entrance to the building so loudly that I jumped. For the first time, Ravenwood didn't feel like my savior. The ambient lighting left shadows in the recesses of the lobby, and the cavernous room felt empty. More than that, as I hurried toward the front door, a shiver went through me, and I was sure that if I looked over my shoulder, someone would be right behind me. I could feel their eyes on me, and my heartbeat sped as I strode across the room, feeling so exposed I wanted to scream.

I was nearly running as I burst out the front doors. Bright, cold sunlight stretched over the lawn, the beautiful light of October contrasting with the shadowy, ominous feeling inside the building. Clutching my jacket tighter against a gust of wind, I started down the steps. I hesitated at the bottom, remembering the headmaster's words.

Not that I felt unsafe walking across campus, but what if he saw me out the window and dragged me back in to lecture me about breaking the rules?

Before I could make up my mind, the door behind me flew open, and a tiny girl with a black pixie cut thundered down the steps, her thick-soled bubble-toe boots hitting each step like a punch. She blew by me and kept running, leaving me standing there gaping.

Had Delilah been spying on my conversation with the dean? Was she mad that I hadn't gotten punished? Or had she been in the building for a different reason?

The hair on the back of my neck stood on end, and I turned slowly, dread weighing like a stone inside me.

"Need an escort?" Alarick asked. He stood on the top step, a smirk on his... *Gawd*... Gorgeous mouth.

"Wouldn't want to make you go out of your way," I muttered.

How had he gotten there? Had he slipped out the door after Delilah, somehow without me seeing him? She'd been loud, but he was freakishly, unnaturally silent. As he padded down the steps, he seemed to barely touch the ground, his footsteps far too soft for such a giant.

He strode down the steps and brushed past me, heading for the girl's dorm. I stood there for a second, unsure of what to do. I had nowhere else to go, and I wasn't stubborn enough to stand here simply to refuse his company.

I started after him, having to run a few steps to catch up. Which then made me feel like an idiot, chasing after him. We walked beside each other for a second, the air charged with discomfort. "No one's going to mess with me right now, anyway," I said, my anger at the administrators returning. "Not if they're smart."

"No one would dare when you're with me."

Annoyance flared inside me, but before I had a chance to voice it, a driving wind sang through the pines in that eerie, mourning wail. I was sure that somewhere far away, I heard a wolf add its lonesome howl to the sound. A cloud swept across the sun, and I pulled my jacket tighter, suddenly glad that Alarick was there. He hadn't actually done anything wrong, had he? He'd warned me to leave, but he hadn't given me a beatdown. Despite his reputation, I didn't know him. Maybe he was perfectly nice. Didn't I owe him at least a chance, the way Svana and Viktor have given me a chance without knowing me?

"I've met your brothers," I said. "I hear you're all super scary and terrible."

Alarick grunted in response.

Annoyed, I couldn't help but goad him. "So, are the rumors true? Are you an asshole?"

"Yeah," he said with another smirk. "I'm an asshole."

Ugh. Nothing worse than someone who wouldn't stoop to my level when I was being petty.

"Good to know," I said lightly.

"What are you so worked up about, anyway?"

"Besides the insufferable company?" I shot back.

The corner of his mouth quirked up. "Yeah, besides that."

"Nothing," I said. We walked in silence for another minute while I replayed the conversation with the headmaster and the dean in my head, getting madder by the second. Finally, it boiled over. Alarick was so quiet, it was hard not to talk. My indignation boiled over, and I let myself vent about the veiled accusations the dean had thrown my way, like I wasn't from around here, so I must be trash. Like I had broken a stupid rule, so I must be a bad person.

"They might as well have said I killed Brooklyn," I finished. "Like I'm capable of murder."

By the time I took a breath, we'd stopped walking. I looked up to find myself outside the dorm. Shit, why had I just told this guy about getting in trouble? For all I knew, the dean had enlisted the Wolf brothers to keep everyone in check, so she didn't have to. I sighed, annoyed with myself and with Alarick for just standing there not saying anything, and turned to go.

"Hey." His massive paw fell on my shoulder, and an explosion of sensation raced through me, and for a second, the brick dorm was gone, and in its place was an enormous wolf staring at me from between rows and rows of pines.

Alarick jerked his hand back like he'd been slapped, and the dorm fell into place before my eyes.

What The. Hell.

"I... Believe you," Alarick blurted. Then he turned and hurried away, shoving his hands in his pockets and tucking his head against the wind. I stood there watching him go, wondering if the Wolf brothers might not be so bad after all.

Chapter Eleven

When I walked into my room, Delilah stepped back from the window, letting the curtain fall back into place. "So," she said, drawing the curtains all the way closed. "You and Alarick Wolf, huh?"

Okay, that was it. I'd had it with this girl. I planted my hands on my hips and glared. "Were you just spying on me?"

She turned from the window, and I immediately felt a pang of regret. Her eyes were bloodshot and puffy, as if she'd been crying. When she'd clomped past me on the front steps, I had thought she was mad. I hadn't realized she'd been crying. And now that she asked about Alarick, it clicked into place. He hadn't just happened to come out after her. He'd followed her out, maybe been with her inside the building.

She'd been crying over Alarick.

"Didn't Svana warn you about them?" Delilah asked, staring at me as she clutched the curtain and glared at me.

"Yeah," I said, tossing my bag onto my bed. "And there's nothing going on between us. He's all yours."

Delilah made a strangled sound, and it took me a second to realize she was swallowing a laugh. "Yeah, right."

"Well, I'm not interested," I said.

Her eyes narrowed. "Because you like Viktor Egilsson," she said, her tone accusing.

"Are we sharing this kind of stuff now?" I asked. "I think you've made it pretty clear we're not going to be friends."

"Right," she said with a sniff. "We're not."

"I mean, I'm okay with starting over," I said. "It would make things a lot easier to live with someone who didn't despise me for no discernible reason. Not to mention someone who likes to spy on me and rat me out to the headmaster."

"I didn't..." She went to her bed, avoiding my eyes, and started gathering up her books.

"Really? You aren't the reason I was called in and bitched out for going hiking?"

"You shouldn't go into those woods," Delilah said. "I did it for your own good."

I planted my feet wide and balled my hands on my hips, standing in front of the door so she couldn't run off without giving me some answers. "Why?"

"Why what?"

"Why shouldn't I go into the woods?"

She slung her backpack over her shoulder but stopped in front of me, eyeing the door at my back. "It's not...safe."

"Why?" I demanded.

She gave an irritated huff. "Those woods belong to Mr. Wolf, and he's a super creep just like his sons. Will that stop you? Probably not. I can tell they've already put their spell on you. You're not going to listen no matter what I say. So maybe I shouldn't even bother to warn you. Go ahead and do whatever you want. Go chasing them around in the woods. Hook up with a Wolf. See what happens."

She pushed past me and yanked open the door, forcing me to stumble forward or be smacked in the back with the door. "I'm going to study in the library with Leigh. So if I disappear, please let someone know that I wasn't planning to run away, and they should definitely investigate."

When she was gone, I flopped onto the bed, frustrated with myself for failing that so hard. It was a relief to have the room to myself, though. Delilah seemed to be always there, filling the room with her unhappiness.

The next night, she was back to her usual glaring and eye-rolling. Nothing notable happened in classes, and no one heard anything about Brooklyn. Since I hadn't known her, it hit me more in the way others reacted. The huddled groups and hushed conversations, the speculation, the way people walked together, hurrying and looking over their shoulders. By the time Friday rolled around, I couldn't wait to sign out and head to Gramma's for the weekend.

*

"You know, there's a full moon tonight," Gramma said, staring out the window with a faraway look in her eyes. Mom said she'd always been eccentric, and sometimes I didn't know if she was acting odd or just being Gramma.

"Is that… Something you celebrate around here?" I asked, trying to simultaneously ask and make a joke. "Because I brought candy to hand out to trick-or-treaters, but I didn't bring anything lunar related."

"Hmm," she said, smiling into the distance.

"I can make dinner," I offered, since she hadn't moved from her rocking chair since I'd arrived. My first week at Ravenwood had been both amazingly wonderful, nerve-wracking, and strange. I was happy to spend a weekend with Gramma handing out candy, watching TV, and sitting around in my sweats. Cooking was a small price to pay for having a refuge away from a weekend with Delilah. Plus, I had loved cooking with Gramma when I was little.

"I'm no chef, but I can whip up some spaghetti," I offered.

"That would be nice, Marla."

I pressed my lips together, not sure of the protocol. Did I tell her I wasn't Mom, or just ignore it?

"Timberlyn," I said at last, laying a gentle hand on her arm. "I'll let you know when dinner's ready."

I stood in the kitchen for a minute, gripping the counter. When we were kids, before Gramma ran off and moved to Canada, we'd gone to her house at Christmas every year. She'd let Josie stand on a chair at the counter beside us while we made cookies. She never cared if we made a mess, or ate half the dough, or if our Christmas cookies looked more like clouds than reindeer and Santas.

When Mom had told us Gramma was "called" to go to Vancouver Island, we hadn't thought she'd buy a house here. But she had, and now I was here, and I needed to make her food.

I got down the pans and made up a batch of spaghetti, listening to her humming in the other room. Things were better after that. We had dinner, and handed out candy, admiring the costumes and pretending to be scared when the ghosts yelled "boo!" We watched *Hocus Pocus* and sang along to the cheesy Halloween songs. Finally, Gramma drifted off to sleep on the couch. I pulled a blanket over her and headed to the guest room.

I lay in bed staring up at the full moon shining through the filmy white curtain on window, wondering what had called Gramma here. Was it the same thing that had called me here?

Of course, that was silly. Ravenwood had called me here. But why?

Now that I thought about it, now that I'd seen Gramma, I wasn't sure that she'd filled out an application from me. And even if she had filled out some kind of interest form, wouldn't a fancy school like Ravenwood want to interview me, or at least have me answer a few essay questions about why I'd be a perfect fit and how I hoped to contribute to the world in my time on earth?

A long, lonesome howl cut through my thoughts, and a chill exploded over my body. I sat up, listening. Another howl came, this one closer. I threw off the covers and climbed out of bed, moving aside the curtain to stare up at the huge silvery-white disk in the sky. I dropped my gaze to the jagged shapes of the pines pointing up at the moon, then lower, tension coiling in my belly as if I already knew what I'd find. When at last my eyes sank to the forest floor, the wolf was waiting, staring back at me.

My wolf.

The thought startled me, but I'd started thinking of him that way at some point. The wolf that visited my dreams, that had seen me in the woods. The wolf with eyes like the boys who shared a last name with it.

As I watched, another wolf appeared beside mine, and then another. They were all staring at me as if they could see me through the window, as if they could see into my soul.

Realizing what I was doing, I jumped back, letting the curtain fall into place. My heart hammered, and I rushed from the room and down the hall, remembering Gramma's unlocked doors. I tiptoed into the living room and leaned over the couch, making sure she still slept soundly, that the howls hadn't woken her. Then I ran to the front door to lock that one, then the back.

I heard another long, mournful howl that sent a pang of loneliness spiraling through me, deep into some secret part of me that I'd kept hidden for so long I'd almost forgotten it was there. The part of me that could feel loneliness, and loss, and sorrow for what I had thought I'd never have. I stood still for a minute, letting the feeling wash over me and into me, burrowing inside my secret heart.

Then I tiptoed back to bed, telling myself it was nothing. Just wild animals. But for a long time, I couldn't sleep because even when I closed my eyes, I saw those big indigo eyes staring back at me, reflecting my own sadness and longing.

*

I woke to the sounds of gulls crying overhead. I sat up slowly, blinking at my unfamiliar surroundings. Trees bent and tossed in the wind overhead. Startled, I jumped to my feet, only to nearly topple over when I stepped on the edge of the blanket wrapped around me.

What's happening? I thought wildly, my mind racing. But then I saw the familiar rocker beside me, and the back door of Gramma's house. My heart began to slow as I scanned the woods and saw nothing. No glowing eyes. No shadows that moved like stalking predators.

I must have come out to watch for the wolves to return, and I'd fallen asleep. Had I seen the wolves last night? Or had it been a dream?

I rubbed my eyes, trying to shake the sluggishness from my mind. Stumbling inside, I carefully folded the faded, patchwork quilt that must have been Grandma's. I couldn't remember taking it out there, or going out there at all, so I had no idea where it had come from. I stowed it in the linen closet, put on a pot of coffee, and zombie-walked to the bathroom.

I had been standing under the spray for at least five minutes, eyes closed and head back, before I woke up enough to look down. Squinting, I blinked in horror at my feet. They were filthy, the toenails broken and blackened with dirt. Sinking onto Gramma's shower stool, I picked up my foot and examined it. The bottom was scraped, with tiny pinprick marks and a few sticky spots of pine sap.

Shit.

I must have sleepwalked around in the woods trying to find the wolves. What was wrong with me? It was one thing to dream about the wolves, remember them in the morning, and draw them. It was another thing entirely to go wandering around in my sleep looking for them. I could have fallen into a ravine or been eaten by, you know, *actual wolves*.

My heart thudding in my chest, I stood again and turned my back to the water. My hands burned, and dread filled my stomach as I turned them over. I had splinters in my palms, and my nails were broken and jagged. Had I seen the things I'd thought were real, or were they part of some delusion? Was I losing my mind?

As I stood under the hot spray, I replayed the moments with the wolves in my mind again and again.

The rumbling growl in the woods the day I'd hiked. The lethal, terrible fangs. The deep blue eyes. And last night, the connection I'd felt staring at that beast, the same connection I felt in my dreams.

I shook my head. I couldn't tell what I had seen and what I had layered with meaning that wasn't there. Had the rumble been only the thunder? Had I conjured an image of a wolf with indigo eyes because of a certain boy with the last name Wolf and familiar, dangerous eyes of the same shade? And if I had, that meant that all my life I hadn't been crazy simply to fulfill the image the other kids at my school had. Maybe it hadn't had anything to do with them except that they'd seen it and separated me out.

Because if I wasn't losing my mind, shouldn't I have been able to tell what I'd seen, what was real, and what wasn't?

Chapter Twelve

Frost squeaked under my combat boots as I hurried across the grass toward Ravenwood's main building a few weeks later. I'd gotten in late from Gramma's the night before, but I didn't think the school was going to punish me for breaking curfew if I was helping an old woman do the overflowing pile of laundry I'd found in her bathroom when I ducked in there on Sunday afternoon to snag a Q-tip.

A group of girls stood a few feet away from the front steps of the building. When I approached, their conversation became both hushed and agitated. A coldness sank into my gut, one that had nothing to do with the icy air. I'd been at Ravenwood less than a month, but I'd already started to believe I'd never feel like a freak again. I hurried up the steps and into the building, trying to forget what I'd just seen. That proved impossible. As I headed to my locker, at least a dozen people moved aside like I was toxic.

A strange thought invaded my mind. Was this how the Wolf boys felt?

Or did they like it, the fear in people's eyes? Maybe it made them feel powerful. I wanted no part of it, and it was only a fraction of the reaction they got. The moment I saw Svana, I swerved aside and grabbed her arm, tugging her toward my locker. "What the hell is going on?" I hissed, ducking my head so no one else would hear.

"Don't you know?" she asked. "Another girl disappeared on Saturday night."

Shock knocked into me, and I had to fight to swallow. "What?"

"Nancy," Svana said. "Nancy from the Netherlands. Did you know her?"

"No," I said, shaking my head. Nancy was in… Actually, almost all of my classes. Though the school was small, I had more than the expected number of classes with the same people. I just assumed they'd grouped me with the other art dorks. Nancy was one of the people in almost all of my classes, but we'd never spoken.

While I got out my books, Svana leaned against the locker next to mine in uncharacteristic silence. She seemed to be mulling over something, staring at the floor until I closed my locker.

"So, where were you on Saturday night?" she asked.

"What?" I asked, pulling back to look at her face. "You can't be serious. You think I killed Nancy? And Brooklyn?"

"Well, no, but…"

"I was at my Gramma's," I said, barely holding in my anger and hurt. I'd thought Svana was my friend, not someone who might suspect me of being a serial killer. "The same place I go every weekend."

"The whole weekend?"

"Yes, the whole weekend," I said through gritted teeth. "I checked out with the office. I can't be the only person who left campus."

"I wasn't saying you did anything wrong," Svana said quickly. "It's just... I guess a lot of people were wondering, and I'm your friend, so I thought I'd ask. So I could tell them to shut up."

Her excuse sounded beyond lame, but then I remembered the dirt on my feet on Halloween, like I'd been wandering in the woods all night. And the splinters in my hands that I still couldn't explain. I pressed my palms against my skirt, glad the marks were long gone. Nothing too strange had happened since Halloween, and I'd almost relaxed. But that was over now.

"Where was she last seen?" I asked carefully, wanting to know but also not wanting to sound like someone who might have killed a girl and was pretending to be innocent.

"Pretty much everyone went out this weekend," she said. "Since it's the last weekend before Thanksgiving. I told you about that, right?"

"Sure," I muttered, though we both knew she hadn't. Another splash of cold water in the face of what I had thought was our friendship. Which was silly, since I'd only known her for a few weeks. Everyone at school hung out on the weekends, and I'd been going home to help Gramma, so it wasn't like I would have gone anyway. But being left out of a party invite, well, it felt a little too reminiscent of when I'd lost all my friends the last time.

"Well, Nancy likes to party, if you know what I mean," Svana said as we made our way down the hall. "She told her roommate that a guy was taking her back to their room, so her roommate stayed overnight with a friend. When she got back on Sunday, Nancy was still gone. By evening, she started to worry. No one's been able to track her down."

"Did someone call her phone?" I said. "Surely they can track her down that way."

Svana shook her head. "Both her and Brooklyn's phones were in their rooms."

"That's weird," I muttered. I had basically zero friends, but I still carried my phone on me most of the time. "Anything else she and Brooklyn had in common?"

"Well, they're both new here this year," Svana said. "And they both disappeared…" She glanced sideways at me and pressed her lips together.

"Since I showed up," I finished.

"You got questioned by the headmaster," Svana said. "Delilah said she overheard them asking you about Brooklyn. This started happening literally the day after you started here, and both times you were off campus when they disappeared. You have to admit it's a big coincidence."

"What the hell?" I demanded, glaring at my flawless friend. "You think I killed two girls? If you think that, just admit it, and we can stop this charade of friendship right now."

Svana hesitated, and that was enough for me. Too much for me.

I turned and stomped past her and another two girls who were whispering together. If I held onto the anger, I wouldn't cry. I marched into my classroom and slung my books onto my desk so hard they slid off the far side.

Appearing out of nowhere, Alarick floated down the aisle and caught them on his way. I closed my eyes and prayed for patience. These boys were not the people I wanted to see right now.

Alarick pushed my books back onto my desk, shuffling them into an approximation of a stack. When he looked up and our eyes met, a shock of memory hit me. Those eyes, so exactly like the wolves I'd seen in the woods. Or in my dreams. Maybe I had fallen asleep and dreamed all of it.

I pressed my nails into the places in my palms where the splinters had been, determined not to let myself believe it wasn't real. The splinters may have been gone, but they'd been there. I may not have seen the wolves in a few weeks, but they'd been there, too. Maybe I was crazy, but I wasn't dreaming.

"How come no one suspects you?" I asked before I could help myself.

Alarick smirked down at me. "I'm above suspicion," he said. "I'm such a model citizen, after all. Keeping peace and order at Ravenwood."

"Or maybe they're scared to accuse you, but they're all thinking it."

Alarick's eyes flashed, and he shoved my books toward me so hard I had to grab them to keep them from flying off my desk all over again. Alarick leaned down, gripping the sides of my desk, his muscles straining against his blazer. "If you don't want things to be worse for you, don't talk to me," he growled. "And stay the fuck away from my brothers."

"Happy to," I snapped. "You're the one standing at my desk."

Alarick pushed back, straightened, and strode to the back of the class. My heart was hammering in my chest, but the moment he was gone, I noticed that every pair of eyes in the room was focused on us. While we talked, it had been like the rest of the world ceased to exist, but now most of the class had filed in, and they were all staring.

Great.

I slid into my seat and focused on straightening my things as if I couldn't feel them all staring. Alarick was right. The last thing I needed was more attention.

I stewed all through class. Had anyone asked Alarick and his brothers where they were the night of the disappearances? Or anyone besides me, for that matter? I'd heard through the gossip mill that on the night Brooklyn disappeared, the boys had said they were together. Did they have an alibi besides each other? If Nancy had left the party with a guy, why were people looking at me when they should be looking for that guy? For all I knew, it could have been Alarick or any of his gang. Hell, it was less likely to be me than any boy in the school. Why weren't they suspicious of Viktor, or even creepy Mr. Underwood himself? He could have pulled the girls aside, lured them to his office by telling them it had something to do with school…

By the time class ended, I didn't trust anyone in the entirety of Ravenwood Academy. I scooped up my books and hurried to my next classes, casting the same suspicious glances at everyone else as they were casting at me and each other.

It wasn't until lunch that I realized I had no one to sit with today. I hurried through the food line and sat at an empty table in the front corner. As if drawn by gravity, my eyes moved to the table of beautiful boys who now sat leaning in, their heads almost touching, engaged in a heated discussion of some sort. Alarick looked even more pissed than usual, and Jose looked like he was about to jump across the table and throttle Donovan.

"Reduced to staring at the hotties," Svana said, appearing in front of me with a small smile.

I didn't know what to say. I couldn't tell if she was making fun of me.

"Can I sit here?" she asked, gesturing with her Diet Coke.

"Okay." I kept my voice neutral, staying on guard.

"Don't think you can get rid of me that easily," she said, plopping down in the empty chair. "Obviously you need me to keep you from turning into one of the Wolfie fangirls."

"Where's Viktor?"

"He's on his way from cooking class," she said. "Listen, I'm sorry about what I said earlier."

Relief washed through me, and I relaxed at last. Maybe she'd been way out of line, but I'd rather have a friend who said too much than none at all. "Me, too."

"Cool," Svana said, taking a swig of her Diet Coke.

"So, do they have any leads?" I asked. "Did anyone see Nancy leave, or did she tell anyone the name of the guy she was leaving with?"

"What are we talking about?" Viktor asked, sliding into the table with a plate laden with a salad and a piece of pizza cooked in the stone oven in the school's fancy kitchen. I finished off my piece with a sigh of pleasure. The food was too good to waste even in the direst circumstances.

"Oh, nothing," Svana said. "How was cooking?"

I stared at Svana, not listening to Viktor's answer. Um, what? Why didn't she want him to know what we were talking about? I was sick of all the secrets, though. I had friends here, but it was like I was always the last to know, always at arm's length.

"Actually, we were talking about Nancy," I said, interrupting Viktor's explanation of some cooking-related assignment.

They both stared at me with identical lavender eyes, like a pair of beautiful dolls.

"Sorry," I said. "But isn't this what everyone should be focused on right now? Why are we just going on like nothing is happening when someone is kidnapping girls from this school? You do realize that means someone here is a literal serial killer?"

"We don't know they're dead," Viktor muttered, looking sufficiently chastised.

"No," I said. "But everyone knows that the chances of finding a missing person are slim, and every day that passes decreases the chances by a huge amount."

They both gaped at me.

"Okay, maybe everyone doesn't know that," I muttered, momentarily distracted by the prickle of heat on my neck. I shot a glance over my shoulder, a little knot of anticipation tightening in my belly before I even saw them. Alarick's eyes met mine, and for a second, I saw something there besides the usual belligerence. Something like…

I shook my head, turning my attention back to my friends. Alarick wasn't concerned about me. I had no reason to be concerned with him.

"How do you know so much about serial killers?" Svana asked.

"I don't," I said. I couldn't tell if the complacence was a Ravenwood thing or a Canadian thing. They were so chill about things here. But didn't everyone know about missing children, and being kidnapped, and the dangers of going off with strange men?

Strange men. That was it.

"Wait," I said. "If Nancy was drunk, would her roommate have let her go off with some guy she didn't know?"

"Her roommate doesn't know who she left with," Svana said. "Nancy didn't tell her. She said Nancy was excited about it and said she'd tell her everything in the morning."

"But she said she was going home with a guy," I said. "Would she have left with someone she didn't know?"

Viktor pushed his plate away, his food untouched as always. I was beginning to think both of my new friends had an eating disorder.

"Probably not," he said.

"Which means it's got to be someone here," I said, a shiver going through me. I glanced over my shoulder at the table near the door where the five thugs sat. Alarick was still watching me, chewing slowly, an intent expression on his face as if he were the one sitting across the table listening to me theorize. A couple girls hovered next to their table, flirting with Adolf, who sat slouched in his chair, smiling up at them.

I turned back, smoothing my hands along my thighs and wondering why my heart was hammering again. Every time I looked at Alarick, my pulse pounded, and butterflies exploded in my belly. My stupid body apparently didn't care a bit what anyone said about them, or even what my mind thought of them.

"My money's on them, too," Viktor said. "I heard a rumor when we first started that they'd killed someone."

"There are lots of rumors about them," Svana said, rolling her eyes. "I've also heard that they beat up the headmaster, or slept with the dean, or slept with every girl in school, or are genetically modified to be so freakishly huge. That doesn't mean all that's true."

"Doesn't mean some of it isn't," Viktor muttered, shooting a dark look at the group. The two girls had perched on Adolf's knees now, and he had an arm around each of them. A weird mixture of jealousy and fear went through me. Where those girls next?

"Is anyone investigating them?" I asked. "Have they been questioned? Has anyone searched their room for clues?"

"They don't have enough evidence to do that to anyone," Svana said, giving me a significant look that said if they'd had evidence, they would have called me in. I watched as Adolf whispered in a girl's ear. She giggled and relayed the message to the other girl while Adolf watched with a hungry look in his eyes. After a second, all three of them got up and left.

"Someone's gotta do it," I said. "If the staff isn't going to, then I'll do some digging myself."

"Are you crazy?" Svana asked, grabbing my arm as I pushed away from the table. Her iridescent pearl nails cut into my arm. "Didn't you hear what Viktor said?"

"What are you going to do?" Viktor asked, his brow furrowing with concern.

I stood and pushed in my chair. "I'm going to get in that room."

Chapter Thirteen

From what I'd heard, all three of the Wolf brothers were players, and none of them were particularly, well, particular. Adolf seemed the most approachable, but he wasn't in class that afternoon. I had a pretty good idea about where he was, and I didn't really want to make their threesome an orgy, so I set my sights on the others. Alarick was the scariest of the bunch, and though we'd had more encounters than I'd had with Donovan, I didn't have any idea what he'd do, or even who he'd be, at any given moment.

That left Donovan and the two friends. The friends seemed less likely than the guys whose dad owned the town, so I fixed on Donovan. If the administration hadn't questioned them, they weren't going to do anything until someone had some evidence. Which meant I had to get some. If I went to them now, pointing fingers with nothing but a gut feeling to go on, it wouldn't just be kids that thought I was crazy at this school.

Not to mention that the admin didn't exactly like me. They probably wouldn't change their opinion of me if I went all psychic detective on their darlings. Maybe that was what the dreams meant. Maybe they were premonitions, and I'd seen the wolves as a symbol of the boys who had committed the murders.

I had my last class right next door to Donovan's, which made it easy to trail behind him. Lots of other students were milling around, so I didn't even have to hide. When I caught sight of Viktor at the bottom of the steps, I waved him over.

"Walk with me?" I asked, threading my arm through his. I didn't want Donovan to get suspicious if he turned around and saw me walking by myself behind him. Not only that, but he might insist on escorting me, the way Alarick had last time.

"What's up?" Viktor asked, smiling down at me as we walked along the stone walkway toward the girls' dorm. Damn it. I had wanted to follow Donovan to his own room, not to his next conquest. But then... What if he was going to find some girl and lure her out into the woods?

"You live in the guys' dorm, right?" I said. "Do you know where their room is?"

Viktor hesitated, swallowing before he answered. His smile disappeared, and he frowned at Donovan's hulking form moving across campus. "Yeah, of course."

"What's your deal with them?" I asked. "I mean, I know they're assholes. Did they beat you up when you were new?"

Viktor pulled his arm from mine. "I just don't like bullies."

"That's all?" I pressed. "Or was it something with Delilah?"

"There was no thing with Delilah."

"I don't know if she'd agree with that."

Donovan had reached the front of the dorm, but he didn't stop. He glanced back over his shoulder once, and when I pretended to be talking to Viktor, he hurried across the grass toward the woods.

"I'm going to follow him," I said.

"No," Viktor said, his hand closing around my arm with surprising strength. "You're not."

"Excuse me?" I said, trying to pry my arm free. "You can warn me all you want, but you can't stop me from going after him."

"Yes, I can," Viktor said, manhandling me toward the dorm.

"What the hell?" I asked, yanking at my arm. "If he can go into those woods, why can't I? What do you know, Viktor?"

"I know that's his dad's property," he said quietly, dragging me through the door of the dorm before releasing me. "He's safe there. You're not."

"Why not?" I asked, rubbing my arm and glaring at him. "Because I'm a girl?"

"Yes," he said. "And I'd rather you not be the next one to disappear."

The seriousness in his tone gave me pause. He didn't just hate the Wolf boys. He was scared of them—really scared. He hadn't just been saying those things at lunch because he didn't like them. He really believed them.

"Fine," I said, crossing my arms over my chest. "I won't follow him. But you have to help me get into one of their rooms."

He hesitated a long moment, then nodded. "Okay."

Delilah walked in just then. She paused and looked from me to Viktor, her eyes narrowing. Then she barreled past in her shit-kicking boots and stomped up the stairs. I stepped back from Viktor, feeling suddenly guilty. "I better go."

"Me, too," he said.

A moment of awkwardness dropped into the space between us. Was I supposed to hug him goodbye? Shake his hand? Wave?

After a pause, he turned on his heel and left the building. I let out a sigh of relief, then climbed the stairs, dread filling me as I went. When I walked in, Delilah was at her spot at the window, watching Viktor go.

"Stalk much?" I asked.

"I thought you said you weren't interested in Viktor."

"I'm not," I said.

I wasn't… Was I?

I shook the thought away. I had much more important things to focus on than whether Viktor could be more than a friend. Girls were dying, and I didn't even know if the school had involved the cops. Were they covering it up so their precious reputation wouldn't be spoiled? Or because they knew exactly who was to blame?

"Have you ever dated one of the Wolf brothers?" I asked. "Is that why you hate them so much?"

"What? No," she said, her eyes widening as she turned from the window and straightened the curtain. I decided her distaste was genuine.

"Why?" I asked, crossing my arms over my chest.

"Because they're complete psychos," she said, looking at me like I was stupid not to know that.

"Other girls don't seem to mind," I said.

"That's their problem." She dropped onto her bed and picked up her earbuds. To my surprise, she hesitated instead of stuffing them into her ears and tuning me out. "Everyone is told to leave them alone when they start here," she said. "If they're smart, they do that. If they're stupid, they go sniffing around. And sometimes, girls disappear. I'm not looking to die, so I don't go sniffing around."

My heart had stopped beating in my chest. "This has happened before?"

"Yeah," she said, raising her chin and staring hard at me, like she expected me to contradict her. "Now, if you don't mind, I have some studying to do."

"Then you know I'm not the one doing it," I said quickly, before she could shut herself up in her laptop.

She looked at me incredulously. "Duh."

"Why do you hate me so much, then?" I asked. "Just because I'm friends with a guy you like?"

Delilah sighed. "I'm not going to make friends with someone who's too stupid to know when to put her head

159

down and leave well enough alone. In case you've never lost someone you care about, here's a hint. It fucking sucks."

With that, she shoved her earbuds in, effectively ending the conversation. Well, that answered that question. It wasn't personal. She didn't think I was crazy, or a freak, or out to get her guy. She just thought I was too stupid to bother with. That I had a death wish, and if she made friends with me, she'd lose a friend.

Maybe she was right, because a minute later, I was in my closet, changing into jeans and hiking boots. I didn't know how long Delilah had been at Ravenwood, but Viktor said it had been a long time, so I was guessing three or four years. That meant that within the last three or four years, someone had disappeared. Maybe more than one someone. Delilah's words hadn't made it clear whether a series of disappearances had happened before, or if just one girl had disappeared. Either way, I had some strange bond with the brothers. When Alarick had touched me, I'd seen something—a row of trees with a wolf between. Maybe that was where he'd buried the bodies.

I couldn't just put my head down, look the other way, and let this continue. It was one thing to avoid bullies and let their reign of terror go on, and another thing to let murderers go unpunished. Maybe I had been called here like Gramma, but it was the wolves who had called me. They had stepped out of my dreams and into my reality, and now I wanted to know why. Was my purpose to stop some teenage psychopaths from murdering girls? Did anyone know anything about these boys, other than their reputation? Did anyone know who they really were, if they were even in high school? They sure as hell didn't look like any high schoolers I'd ever seen.

I threw on a jacket and headed out. This time, I didn't just text my sister. I also texted Svana and Viktor.

"I'm going into the woods after Donovan. If I don't show up tomorrow, please know that I didn't run away. Thank you for being my friends."

I told my sister that something weird was going on, and that I wasn't in trouble, but if anything happened to me, she should get the American authorities involved and not let them quit until they'd figured it out. Then, I took a deep breath and turned to the woods. A dense, wet fog had sprung up between the trees, and there was no sign of Donovan Wolf.

I had nothing but a hunch to go on, but I was sure that the disappearances had something to do with these creepy woods. I was sure that there was something strange going on with me and these boys. So, I started out at a brisk pace. In minutes, the fog had swallowed me. My skin was slick with it, my hair damp, and I could hardly see ten feet in front of me. At first, I thought I could make out a spot here or there where the pine needles had been disturbed, but all too soon I'd lost his trail, if there was one.

I visualized where I was as I walked, so I wouldn't get lost. Not that I ever got lost. Somehow, I didn't think being exceptionally gifted at finding my way around had gotten me that Ravenwood invitation. Now that I was here, I didn't want to leave, but I still didn't understand how I'd gotten accepted at all. And the Wolf boys definitely hadn't called me here. That was a silly thought. They had made it clear that they didn't want me here. It must be the lost girls.

I mulled it over as I walked. Gramma lived on the edge of Ravenwood Forest, but she was in the next town over. Which meant this forest was pretty big—I was guessing it had to be at least five miles until I'd reach her town. This whole thing was apparently owned by Mr. Wolf, though I had no way of knowing when his property ended. Did he own the woods that ran up to the back of Gramma's yard? Would his sons really come to her back door and howl?

What was I even thinking? These guys were scary, maybe even murderers, but they were people, not wolves. I almost laughed at myself for letting my mind wander to that thought. Yep, I was definitely losing it if I'd begun to associate the Wolf boys with the actual wolves who had appeared in my dreams. Believing the same wolves from my dreams had appeared in my real life was crazy enough.

I didn't need to go adding to it. Because if I was that crazy, if I could sleepwalk and not remember anything the next day, what if I really could have done something to those girls?

Suddenly, a figure materialized out of the fog. I nearly screamed as I stumbled backward. Emerging from the swirling white, Alarick seized me by the throat and slammed my back against a tree. I gasped for breath, still reeling with shock as he towered over me, his dark eyes both beautiful and deadly.

"What the fuck are you doing on our property?" he growled, his voice sharp with hatred.

"Nothing," I managed, squirming in his grip. His hand was so enormous that it covered my entire neck, his fingers wrapped around my throat with so much pressure I nearly choked.

"That's right," he said. "You aren't doing anything because you're leaving. And you won't be coming back."

I grabbed his hand, trying to pry his fingers loose, but they were like iron. "What are you so afraid of?" I demanded.

Alarick's lip pulled into a disdainful sneer. "I'm not afraid of you, puny human."

"Then why are you so threatened by me?" I asked, kicking out at his legs. He didn't even seem to feel my thick hiking boots striking his shins. "You didn't want me at Ravenwood, you don't want me hiking in the woods. Why am I so scary to a big man like you?"

I knew I should shut up, but fear had the words rushing out of me.

Alarick leaned closer, his blue eyes like a sea at twilight, a sea I could drown in and be lost forever. His warm breath caressed my cheeks, and suddenly, my traitorous heart was thumping for new reasons, reasons I'd never had before. I couldn't tell if I was more terrified that he'd hurt me or that he'd draw back. The scent of him invaded me, dowsing the fight in me and replacing it with bewilderment. He smelled like pine trees and wind, fierce and wild, the kind of wind that pierced the skin and sent waves smashing against the ocean's jagged shore.

"You don't scare me," he said, his voice low. "Do I scare you?"

"Yes," I whispered, my fingers still wrapped around his wrist, though I wasn't fighting anymore. I was... Waiting. For what, I wasn't sure.

"Good," he said, his eyes narrowing. "You should be scared of me. My father owns this property. He hunts here. Accidents happen. You wouldn't want to be caught creeping around in the fog like this, trespassing on our property. Bad things happen to girls who do that."

Terror surged inside me, and I yanked in vain against him, kicking and clawing. He'd done it. He might as well have admitted it. The psycho watched me squirm like a butterfly under a pin for a minute before loosening his grip. I tore myself free and leapt clear of him, only then turning to face him. My heart was racing, my breath coming fast.

"What kind of coward comes out here just to beat up a girl?" I wanted to spit in his eye, to tear his face off, but I wasn't about to get that close.

He chuckled, which only made my fury spike higher. "I didn't beat you up," he said. "It won't even leave a mark."

"Let me get you trophy," I said. "Congratulations, you didn't strangle me."

Alarick just smirked at me. "Let me make this simple for you. You're out of line. My job is to keep order. Which means I'm here to make you fall in line."

"Good luck with that," I shot back.

"Then let me put it this way. We own this property. Anything on this property is ours. We'll claim it any way we see fit."

A knot of coldness settled in my belly, sending a chill through my entire body. The heat of my rage was extinguished, and all I wanted was to get the hell out of there. But I had one last thing to say. "So, anything that's in my house is mine," I said. "Even a blanket I've never seen before?"

Alarick's eyes narrowed, his nostrils flaring as fury built in his eyes like a thundercloud. That's when I knew. Somehow, some way, he had been the one to put me on the back porch on Halloween night. That wasn't Gramma's blanket. It was his blanket. And somehow, he'd lured me out of the house and done… God, I didn't even want to know what he could have done to me.

But I couldn't *not* know, either.

"It was you," I hissed, anger pulsing in my temples again. "What did you give me? Did you drug me?"

"Shut up," he growled. "You don't know what you're talking about."

"You're right. I don't. Because you gave me something so I wouldn't remember. Didn't you? What makes me so special, Alarick? Why didn't you just kill me like the other girls?"

"Shut. Up." He ground the words out, and I knew I was making him mad, too. And as much as a part of me relished that, because I wanted him to be as angry as I was, I wasn't stupid enough to provoke a guy who was literally twice my size and ten times as strong.

"I'll stay quiet like a good little girl if you tell me the truth," I said.

"You were sleepwalking," he said. "That's what happened. I wrapped you in a blanket and brought you home."

"It was you," I said, my voice conveying the wonder of it. I'd suspected, known somewhere deep inside, but part of me had believed I was as crazy as everyone had always thought. But I wasn't crazy. And despite all his faults, Alarick hadn't kidnapped me. He'd taken me home, even put his own blanket around me. Maybe he wasn't the monster everyone thought, just like I hadn't been the one everyone back home saw when they looked at me. I knew better than to make assumptions or believe the rumors, and yet, he hadn't done much to prove them wrong.

He lifted his head, his nostrils flaring again, as if he were scenting the air, seeing through the fog somehow. When his gaze dropped to me again, his smirk had returned, but there was a tightness around his eyes. "You'd better run," he said in a taunting tone that didn't reach his troubled gaze. "Someone might catch you alone in the woods with the Big Bad Wolf. You don't want the reputation of being that kind of girl, now do you?"

Just when I'd started to give him the benefit of the doubt.

"Maybe you should worry about your own reputation if the fact that being seen with you can give a girl a bad name," I shot back.

"I have bigger things to worry about than what people think of me," he said. "And you will, too, if you don't get out of here."

Before I could ask what that meant, I heard a snapping behind me. An image of the wolf's long, deadly teeth flashed into my mind, and I spun around, shrinking back toward Alarick as if he suddenly offered protection rather than more danger. I could hear footsteps now, only barely audible through the blanket of thick fog.

"Who's there?" I asked, my voice quavering horribly. I took a step back, but when I glanced over my shoulder, I found myself alone. Only swirling white remained where Alarick had stood just moments before.

Chapter Fourteen

I backed against the tree where Alarick had pinned me, my fingers clutching the bark behind me as if it could anchor me. Absurdly, I wished for Alarick to appear again. Sparring with him was better than whatever else was in these woods.

The fog parted, and a familiar figure stepped through. I let out a breath of such relief I almost collapsed on the ground.

"Viktor," I said. "Oh my god, you scared me. What are you doing out here?"

He looked almost as startled as I felt, but the expression quickly changed to match my own relief. "There you are," he said. "I was looking for you."

"Really?" I asked, then realized how desperate and fangirlish I sounded, like I'd hoped he would come after me. I hadn't. I'd just sent the text in case I disappeared.

"Yeah," he said. "Why else would I be out here, trespassing where I don't belong and I'm not wanted?"

I realized then that my question had come across as incredulous to his ears. He thought I didn't believe that's why he was in the woods. I wasn't actually sure what I thought. He'd looked startled when he saw me, but maybe just because he'd seen nothing but trees, and then suddenly I'd appeared through the fog just as he'd appeared to me. Or maybe he'd been in the woods for some other reason…

"You didn't have to do that," I said. "I didn't mean for you to do that."

"I was—we were worried about you."

"Well, thanks," I said. "I'm fine. But let's go back. This fog is even creepier than the woods."

I wasn't sure if Viktor was part of the reason I felt so cold and jumpy, or if it was just the woods, the fog, and Alarick's warnings. I just knew that I was done with playing psychic detective for the day, and that I wanted to get out of there as fast as possible.

"You said you wouldn't follow him," Viktor said as we started back toward the academy. Despite the fog, I was sure of exactly where to go. My internal compass never failed me.

"I know," I said. "I just... I got in a fight with Delilah, and I needed to clear my head." I felt bad lying to him, and I wasn't even sure why I didn't want him to know I'd talked to Alarick. Maybe just because he'd be mad, and he hated Alarick, but I wasn't sure. At least part of what I'd said was true. I had fought with Delilah, and that's what had made me change my mind about following Donovan.

I waited for Viktor to lecture me, to tell me all the things the dean had said. The things Delilah and everyone else seemed to believe. I'd been trespassing, and the Wolf family was prominent, and if anything happened to me, they'd be justified in whatever they did. Even if I found something, no one would believe me. That if I didn't fall in line, I was asking for it, and did I have a death wish?

But he didn't. He only asked if I needed a coat, which I refused, since I already had my leather jacket. We made it back to the dorm, and again, an awkward moment of indecision hung between us. Then we both started to speak at once.

"Timberlyn, listen," he said at the same moment that I said, "Goodnight."

I gave a nervous laugh. "Thanks for coming to find me."

"Yeah," he said, a frown creasing his beautiful brow. "Thanks for texting me. If anything had happened to you…" He shook his head.

"Luckily you were there to rescue me," I joked, trying to get a smile out of my serious friend. Now that he'd walked me back to the academy, I felt like shit for wondering about his motives. Delilah had already told me that this had happened a few years ago, and Viktor hadn't even been here then.

"We should get inside," he said. "It's almost dark, and we're not even supposed to be out this late."

I noticed then that evening had mostly obscured the woods, with only ghostly traces of trees visible through the fog. No one else was about. If Viktor had wanted to harm me, he could have done it in the woods. I had to stop being so paranoid. He and Svana were my friends. They weren't going to stab me in the back. Trust was a lesson I was finding harder to learn than I'd expected.

I was about to head inside when I heard someone call out in the woods. I froze, my eyes widening as I checked with Viktor. This time, no one called me crazy. His head had whipped around toward the woods, his shoulders tensed. I squinted into the gathering darkness in the woods, sure I'd heard a male voice call out an all-too-familiar name.

"You heard that?" I asked, my heart in my throat, not daring to say her name in case I was wrong. I had enough marks against me. I didn't want anyone to know I hallucinated as well as appeared just as other girls began to go missing.

Before Viktor could answer, the soft thud of footfalls in the pines sounded, and the next moment, a dirty, naked girl came flying out of the shadowy woods, the fog trailing behind her like groping fingers trying to suck her back in.

"Brooklyn," I gasped, though she was hardly recognizable. I'd only seen her one day, and her long brown hair was now tangled and matted instead of shiny and sleek, but I was sure it was her. I raced forward as she fell to all fours, her hair obscuring her face.

"Call 911," I called back to Viktor, who hadn't recovered from the shock enough to move yet. I knelt beside the girl, who was filthy and shivering. Her hands were black with grime, her nails torn and bloody.

"Brooklyn," I said, trying to keep my voice calm even though I was shaking, and my head was reeling with a million panicked thoughts. "We're going to get you some help. You're safe."

"I don't think there's 911 here," Viktor said, crouching beside me. "I called Dr. Underwood, the infirmary, and the campus security. They're on their way."

He reached out like he was going to put a hand on Brooklyn's shoulder, then thought better of it and drew back. Instead he slid his arm around me, and as selfish as it was, I was relieved for the comforting touch.

"We have campus security?" I asked, sinking into his embrace.

"One guy," he said. "Everyone says he has the easiest job on earth because the Wolf posse does the actual work for him. He just sits in his office playing Minecraft all day."

"Brooklyn?" I asked gently. "Do you want a blanket?"

Her body began to shake, but it wasn't shivering. It was violent shudders wracking her body. Her head snapped up, her eyes filled with so much rage it blazed out at me like missiles. "Leave me alone," she screamed, her voice hoarse but incredibly strong. She leapt to her feet and took off sprinting across the dying grass.

Viktor cursed quietly and leapt to his feet. "Go inside where you're safe. I'll get her."

Before I could protest, he dashed into the fog lying heavy over the campus like an obscuring blanket. I shivered, glancing back over my shoulder at the woods. The woods where someone was calling Brooklyn, maybe chasing her, maybe not wanting her to reach the safety of the school grounds.

I glanced up at the comforting glow of the light in my second-floor window. How easy it would be to just go inside, to huddle under the blankets and let everyone else do the work.

But I hadn't come to Ravenwood to hide away and cower in my room. I'd come for a chance to stop cowering. Taking a deep breath, I turned and jogged after Brooklyn. I couldn't see her or Viktor, and it seemed like a long minute before I heard his voice murmuring to her through the fog. I caught sight of flashlight beams sluggishly fighting through the dense cover, and I ran toward them.

Four figures emerged from the fog behind the lights. A tall, slender woman accompanied by a short man with a clipped, scurrying gait. A few steps away lumbered a tall, fat man, and beside him was an elderly woman tottering across the grass in heels. They found Viktor's voice and stopped, all of us arriving almost simultaneously.

The older woman stooped beside Brooklyn while Dr. Rowe seemed more interested in me. "What are you kids doing out here this time of night?" she asked, suspicion and accusation coloring her words as she glared.

"I went over to see Timberlyn," Viktor said, standing from Brooklyn's side. "She came outside to talk to me in private. We were just outside her dorm when Brooklyn came running out of the woods."

Dr. Rowe surveyed my attire, from my leather jacket with water beaded on it from the fog to my dirty, wet hiking boots. "You just stepped out of your dorm to talk to Mr. Egilsson?" she asked.

I fought the urge to glance at Viktor. Despite his apparent acceptance of the status quo, he'd come out to find me in the woods, trespassing and maybe putting himself in danger, and now he was lying to cover for me. I decided right then I was never going to be suspicious of him again.

"Yes," I said to Dr. Rowe, holding her gaze without backing down.

If we both lied, how could she prove otherwise?

The answer to that appeared not a second later. The fog parted, and Alarick's towering figure stepped through. Unlike when I'd seen him, he was wearing nothing but a pair of low-slung jeans, and even though it was a completely inappropriate time, I couldn't help but gulp when I took in his chiseled abs, broad muscular shoulders, and sculpted chest. His skin glimmered with a golden tan as the flashlight beams cut across him in the dark.

Then he crouched beside Brooklyn, and I remembered why we were all here. Had he been the one who called out to Brooklyn in the woods? It had been a quick cry from a distance off, and I couldn't tell if it had been him or not.

"Brooklyn, you need to get it together," he said in a firm but gentle voice.

Indignation rose inside me. Who said that to a girl who had obviously been traumatized, and probably kidnapped by him and his psycho brothers? Now I was sure it was him who had called to her, trying to keep her from getting back here. And yet, none of the adults were questioning him on his whereabouts. No one was asking why he was out here half naked, or why Brooklyn was naked. He obviously hadn't taken the shirt from his back to give to her when he found her in the woods.

"I've got her," he said in that same low, commanding voice. The nurse backed off, and Alarick scooped Brooklyn into his arms and stood. She didn't fight, but instead turned her head into his broad, strong chest and clung to his neck.

I waited for someone to say something, for the nurse to tell him she needed a hospital or that she could lie down in her office. But no one said anything.

And then Donovan stepped out of the fog. He was also barefoot, but he wore a plaid shirt with a few of the buttons undone or buttoned crookedly over his jeans.

"Where's Adolf?" Alarick asked him.

"Coming," Donovan said. "She okay?"

"We'll take her to the infirmary," Alarick said, his eyes cutting to me with a meaningful weight. "They can get her fixed up."

Suddenly, I had a feeling they were all in on something with the admin, something I didn't know and wasn't supposed to find out.

"Yes, we'll get her taken care of," Dr. Underwood said, licking his lips quickly. "Let's get her inside."

Adolf appeared just then, swaggering up with his usual dickish confidence. "We can take care of this," he said. "She's fine."

"You mean they can take care of it," Alarick said, cutting his eyes to me with that same weighted stare.

Adolf spared me a haughty smirk before turning to his brothers. "Sure, whatever," he said. "She'll know soon enough."

"Know what?" I burst out. "What are you guys talking about? Why are you even here?"

"She was running through our woods, wasn't she?" Alarick said. "We know when someone's on our property."

He stared me down, his eyes a threat. He'd rat me out, the bastard. If I made a fuss now, he'd tell the admin I'd been off school grounds, that I'd been trespassing.

But fuck that. I wasn't keeping quiet just to save my ass. Not if Brooklyn had been held hostage on that property.

"Why isn't anyone freaking out?" I asked, throwing out an arm toward the admin. "A girl has been missing for almost a month, and she shows up obviously in bad shape, like maybe she's been kidnapped? And you're all just standing there like it's no big deal? What is wrong with you?"

"Calm down, Timberlyn," Viktor murmured beside me.

"Don't tell me to calm down," I said. "I'm the only one acting normal here. You should all be freaking out! There should be authorities here, and psychologists, and trauma counselors, and... And... You're all just acting like these three assholes are going to fix all your problems like they always do."

"Aww, thanks," Adolf said. "I'm flattered."

"That wasn't a compliment," I growled.

"Could have fooled me," he said with a shrug.

"Come on," Alarick said to the nurse, and he started off across the grass.

"Where are you taking her?" I called after him. "Back to your sick torture dungeon in the woods?"

"You've got a kinky imagination," Adolf said. "I like it."

I pushed past him and jogged after Alarick. Viktor called after me, but I had to know where they were taking her. If I couldn't do anything right now, at least I'd be a witness. I could make sure they were really taking her to the infirmary and not somewhere else—like back into the woods.

"You know, I could fix your problems, too," Adolf said, keeping pace with me.

"What?"

"You said we fix all Ravenwood's problems," he reminded me. "I can fix yours, too. I know just what you need."

"Let me guess. You think I need you."

"Well, that's a given," he said. "But what you really need is to relax a little. Don't worry, a lot of girls have that problem. And like all the other problems, I'm here to solve that one."

I couldn't help rolling my eyes. "How generous of you."

"I like to think so," he said. "I provide a service. You need to get laid, I'm here to do the job. Guaranteed to help you sleep at night."

"Thanks, but no thanks."

"Come on, Timberlyn. When was the last time you got laid?"

"I'm fifteen," I said. "It's not like I'm having a dry spell."

"So, you've never gotten laid? Yeah, you definitely need it."

"Can we focus on the kidnapping right now?" I asked, hurrying to get away from him and back to Brooklyn. He was getting me flustered with all these personal questions.

"You know, I can give you the virgin special," he said. "It's not a problem. I think they even excuse you from class the next day. You know, to recover."

"Kind of like Brooklyn is recovering right now?" I asked. "Stop trying to flirt with me, you psycho. In case you didn't notice, the girl who's been missing just showed up, and she looks like she needs more than your crude lines to help her."

We arrived at a small door off one wing of the building. Above it was the word "Infirmary," so at least I knew Alarick wasn't taking her back into the woods. In fact, he was murmuring to her in a comforting way as the nurse unlocked the door. Alarick carried her inside, and Donovan pushed past me and into the room as well. I tried to step inside, but Donovan turned and pressed a hand to my chest, holding me back.

"Go home," he said, his voice low and hard.

"What?" I asked, jerking away from his hand. "No way. I have to make sure she's okay."

"You can't help her," he said. "And you're not family. You have no reason to be here."

"Neither do you," I shot back as Adolf stepped past his brother into the room.

"Go home, Timberlyn," Donovan said again. "There's nothing you can do."

"Is that what you're going to tell the hospital tomorrow? That there was nothing more you could do?"

"Egilsson," he called into the fog. "Come take care of this... Problem."

"What are you doing to her?" I demanded.

"We're doing everything we can to help her."

He was either a sociopath and the world's best liar, or he was sincere, because his eyes were earnest, even kind as they locked on mine.

"Come on," Viktor said quietly, his hand sliding around my elbow and tugging me back. "The nurse is there. We'd just be in the way."

I was shaking and on the verge of tears as the door closed in my face. I wasn't sure what else I could have done, but there had to be something. I couldn't break down the door or wrestle my way past one of the giant boys in that room, but there must be something. I vowed as I walked back to my dorm in silence, escorted by an equally silent Viktor, that if I couldn't help, at least I'd find some way to avenge her.

Chapter Fifteen

The next day, the school was buzzing. Everyone had heard that Brooklyn was back, though she wasn't in class. Speculation ran wild as people guessed where she'd been, what had happened to her, and what she'd be like now. They wanted answers, and I was glad for her that she wasn't there for the nosy kids to ask. Still, I wanted answers myself. I wanted to know where she was and that she was safe.

Unfortunately, I didn't get a chance to ask. Though Ravenwood Academy didn't have Thanksgiving break, since they were Canadian, my parents insisted that I needed to come home for a break. I got excused from the headmaster and headed home for the next week. Svana assured me via text that Brooklyn was back at school and appeared relatively healthy. In truth, it was a relief to get away and put Ravenwood out of my mind for a few days, to play Mario Cart with my sister and eat too much stuffing.

By the time I returned to Ravenwood Academy, everything seemed to have gone back to normal... Sort of.

When I got to science class, I was surprised to find my seat beside Adolf had already been taken. A girl I barely recognized sat there, and it took me a second to realize it was Brooklyn. Instead of returning to her shiny-haired friends, she'd taken my seat next to Adolf. I glanced around, sure that everyone would be staring and whispering the same way they had when I'd sat next to him. But no one paid them any mind.

I found the seat vacated by Brooklyn and slid into it, earning a few curious glances from her former friends. I peeked over my shoulder at her. She'd cleaned up since the night we'd found her. Her hands were no longer stained black, and her nails were short but clean. Her hair was still a bit frizzy, as if she'd stopped caring about using the right product or even running a brush through it. She wore no makeup, and her uniform looked wrinkled and slightly dingy as she slumped in her chair. Adolf sat beside her, but she paid no attention to him. She stared straight ahead with a sullen, bored expression on her hollow-eyed face.

I didn't know what to do, so I turned to my neighbor when the teacher started in on her lesson. After all, Brooklyn had been her friend *before*.

"Have you talked to Brooklyn?" I whispered.

The girl, Amy, looked surprised for a second, and I tensed up, ready for her to tell me to go die in a hole like the popular girls at home would have done. But she ducked her head and leaned closer. "I tried, but she won't talk to anybody but *them*."

She jerked her head back toward where Brooklyn and Adolf sat, but I already knew exactly who she meant. "She sat there by choice?" I asked.

"Svana said it's probably because they found her," Amy said. I was surprised for a second, but then I realized that at a school this small, everyone knew everyone else. Svana liked gossip and being in the middle of things. She was probably speculating along with everyone else, though I hadn't had time to ask for all the details yet.

"Does she talk to Viktor?" I asked. I was about to add that he'd been there, too, but then I changed my mind. I didn't know what he wanted people to know. I wondered, though. Would she talk to me? If I tried, and she wouldn't, then Svana's theory was wrong. What the hell had they done to her? Was it some kind of brainwashing? Stockholm Syndrome?

I didn't have a chance after class. When the bell rang—which was an actual bell outside that someone had to ring, like an old church—I started to get up, but Amy grabbed my arm and pulled me back down. "They go first," she said.

Adolf got up and picked up Brooklyn's books. "Come on," he said. "You first."

She gave him a resentful pout but stood and stomped down the row of seats to the door, Adolf following close behind. He opened the door and then turned back to the class. "You can go now."

With that, he and Brooklyn disappeared out the door, leaving me gaping while everyone else scrambled to get their books.

"What was that?" I asked.

"It's been like that since she came back," Amy said. "He told us to stay in our seats until she was out."

"And everyone just did it?" I asked. "The teacher didn't say anything?"

Amy shrugged and finished gathering her books. "What's the point? Besides, I don't want to make Adolf mad."

"You think he'd hurt you at school?" I asked, making my way out of class with her.

She gave me a look like I was nuts. "No, of course not," she said. "I'm still hoping I'll get another night with him before this year ends. I mean, it only happened one time, but what a night it was." She smiled dreamily, staring off into space as we walked down the hall. I wanted to laugh, but I couldn't tell if she was kidding or not.

Finally I said, "That good, huh?"

"You have no idea," she said with a sigh. "But I hear he won't do repeats until he's had a chance with every girl at school. But then Kaitlyn was telling me that it's not every girl, it's just the new ones. Have you had a chance?"

"Um, no thanks," I said. "Not interested."

"You're missing out," she sang as she swept off down the hall toward her next class.

I headed to art. Usually, I didn't pay much attention to Donovan, but today my eyes scanned the room for him. He was already in his back corner seat, alone at a rectangular table with a large sketchbook lying in front of him. Taking a deep breath, I made my way back and took the seat diagonal from him at the table.

He glanced up, his eyes darkening when he saw me. "We were hoping you wouldn't come back."

"Wow," I said. "I guess you're a nice guy just like your brothers."

His jaw worked back and forth, and then he went back to his paper. I checked out his work from the corner of my eye, disappointed to find only an abstract with lots of angles and sharp edges. I opened my own sketchbook, scolding myself for thinking I'd get information that easily. What had I expected—a drawing of the missing girls chained up in his basement?

I turned to the page I'd worked on before my trip home, something I'd done the morning after one of the nightmares. Right now, it was just a figure, but I knew who it was. It was his brother, though I'd never dreamed of him exactly. I'd dreamed of my wolf. And somehow, that had become Alarick.

I filled in the eyes, as dark as the ocean and as bright as gemstones. I didn't want to draw Alarick in the middle of class, though. Everyone would know who it was.

Instead, I elongated the fingers on each hand, drawing long, razor claws extending from the end of each one. Then I added a ruff of fur to each cheek, making it look like one of the shaggy werewolves from a bad movie.

"What are you drawing?" Donovan asked.

"A monster," I said lightly. "Know anything about that?"

I didn't know why I couldn't stop provoking them. I knew I was poking a beast, but I couldn't contain my curiosity about them. I had to know. More than that, I couldn't stand them having so much power, thinking they ran the world. If I couldn't unseat them from their thrones, maybe I could at least unsettle them. I could be the earthquake that shook the ground their thrones sat on, make them sweat a little.

"Where'd you get that idea?" Donovan asked, staring at me so intently I was the one unsettled. Not that I was going to let him see it.

"From my dreams," I said, beginning to draw a long, curved fang in the man's mouth. "I see a lot of things in my dreams. Sometimes they seem so real I almost believe them." I looked up then, meeting Donovan's eyes and holding them. I was daring him to say something, but more than I wanted him to deny it, I wanted him to tell me the truth about Halloween night. I wanted it so bad it nearly turned my heart inside out. If they were really behind the girls disappearing, why had they taken me home that night? If they'd found me wandering in the woods, sleeping, I was the easiest prey they'd ever find. Why had they taken me home?

And if they had, and they weren't responsible for the girls going missing, then who was?

Only one person knew the answer to that for sure. I just had to find a way to talk to her when she wasn't being escorted by one of the Wolf brothers. It wasn't an easy feat. At lunch, she sat with them. Her trauma definitely hadn't taken her appetite. In fact, after she ate her lunch, she grabbed Alarick's plate and started scarfing down the food while Adolf laughed his ass off. Alarick punched him in the shoulder so hard Adolf fell out of his chair, after which he went to get another plate. He came back with a heaping helping of mutton and potatoes, which Alarick swiped, ate half of, and passed on to Brooklyn.

"She's going to get fat if she doesn't stop eating like that," Amy commented as we headed out of the cafeteria.

"I don't think she has anything to worry about," Svana said. She'd been able to fill me in on what I'd missed, which wasn't much. Brooklyn hadn't come back for a few days, and then she'd hung out with the Wolf posse and refused to talk to anyone else.

I couldn't get a moment with her for the rest of the week or the next, either. She was always in class when I got there, and Adolf either told everyone to sit while he escorted her out, or he left class early with her. The teacher never batted an eye to any of it. At lunch, she sat with the five guys, who watched with expressions ranging from approval to amusement as she inhaled impossible amounts of food for such a small person. She no longer slept in the girls' dorm, although it was supposedly not permitted to stay the night in the guys' dorm. Apparently, that was another rule the Wolf boys were allowed to break.

I found myself wondering which of their rooms she slept in, and an unexpected flare of jealousy rose inside me at the thought of her sharing Alarick's bed. I hadn't felt anything like that when Amy mentioned sleeping with

Adolf, but I had something different with Alarick. Maybe it was all in my imagination, my dreams, but there it was. I somehow knew him in a way I didn't understand no matter how much I meddled and pondered.

A week before Christmas break, I'd nearly given up on talking to Brooklyn when I had to stay a couple minutes late to finish up an art project. As I headed down the empty hall afterwards, I saw Alarick leaning against the wall, his massive arms crossed over his chest. My mind took a quick detour to check out those broad shoulders, the bulge of his muscles straining against his uniform. Then I noticed what he was doing. Standing outside the girls' bathroom as if he were guarding it. My heartbeat sped as I realized what that meant. Brooklyn was in there.

I increased my pace, nearly running by the time I reached the door.

"You can't go in there."

His voice was so commanding I screeched to a halt even though my imaginary emergency had almost convinced me it was real. "I have to go," I said. "I can't wait."

"Use the men's."

"Can't," I said, shoving open the door and darting in. I glanced over my shoulder, expecting him to follow, but the door remained closed. I ducked into a stall and pulled the door closed. I did my business and came out at the same time as Brooklyn. She went straight to the sink, her eyes downcast. As she washed her hands, I lowered my voice to a whisper.

"Are you free to talk?" I asked.

She didn't answer.

"Are the Wolf boys still keeping you captive somehow?" I glanced at the door, as if afraid Alarick might somehow hear my soft whisper over the running water and through a closed door.

"Leave me alone," Brooklyn said without looking up.

"Okay," I said. "I'll leave you alone. But if you change your mind, come to me, okay? I'll find some way to help you. I promise."

She turned off the water and gripped both sides of the sink, leaning forward so her hair obscured her face. A low, hoarse moan came from somewhere deep inside her, almost like a growl.

"Brooklyn?" I whispered, reaching out to touch her shoulder blade. "How can I help?"

Her head whipped up and toward me. "You can't," she screamed at the top of her lungs, her voice so loud it twisted into something grotesque against the tile walls. I cringed against the volume of her voice as it assaulted my ears, but it wasn't just her raging voice that made me withdraw. Her eyes flashed with so much hatred that I stumbled back a step. The bathroom door flew inwards, and Alarick leapt across the room at the same moment that Brooklyn leapt at me. His arm whipped around her middle, and she folded almost double, her nails raking down the sleeve of my leather jacket as she tried to get to me. Furrows tore into the leather.

"I knew not to fucking trust you," Alarick snarled at me, the fury in his eyes matching Brooklyn's. "You can't just take a piss like a regular person. You have to meddle."

Brooklyn let out a horrible, snarling noise, and Alarick spun from me, holding Brooklyn toward the door. "Calm down," he said to her, his voice gentle and soothing, the furthest thing from the hate-filled tone he'd used with me. "I got you. It's okay, Brook."

Hearing him croon softly to her made my heart nearly crack. He wasn't holding her hostage. He obviously cared about her. And here I was, some girl she didn't even know, prying into her business. What had I been thinking? Alarick was right about me. I was ignorant and couldn't stop meddling in things I didn't understand.

Tears clogging my throat, I ran past them and out of the bathroom, vowing that from now on, I'd just accept the status quo like everyone else and stop looking for trouble. I wouldn't think about the way Brooklyn's eyes had changed color, or the way her teeth had looked sharp, or the fact that her nails had sliced through my leather jacket like blades. Everyone had been right all along. If I didn't want to get hurt, I'd better keep my head down and mind my own business.

Chapter Sixteen

Snow fell, and the temperature dropped, but it wasn't the bitter cold I'd expected from winter in Canada. It melted quickly, and the days were brisk but sunny as students hurried around the commons. With Brooklyn back, no one seemed to remember that the second girl to disappear had never come back. We went to classes and usually walked in pairs, but no one commented if someone walked alone.

I tried to stay out of the way of the Wolf boys and their friends, now including Brooklyn. I sat with Svana and Viktor, and in science, I sat with Amy instead of Adolf. I didn't bother Donovan in art class, and I ignored

Alarick, Vance, and Jose entirely. Soon enough, it was time to go home for Christmas break.

This time, Gramma came with me. We all ate a lot, exchanged gifts, and hung around in our pajamas for an inexcusable amount of time. It was almost enough to make me forget the weirdness of school. Almost enough to make me believe everything was in my head, and that life was still normal. Except for a few dreams, the break was the vacation that every ordinary freshman had.

All too soon, it was time to go back to Ravenwood. And even though I'd been accepted there, though I'd made friends and was no longer a freak, I was still filled with dread at the prospect of returning. No matter what anyone said, things at the school just weren't right. It wasn't normal. Girls didn't have fingernails that could cut through leather. People didn't ignore when a girl went missing. A school didn't let its own student body run things.

Except at Ravenwood, all that was commonplace.

The first week back, everything was as it had been before, until I almost started to believe all that was normal. That weekend, I went home to Gramma's as usual.

We were standing on the back porch drinking tea on Saturday night when Gramma said, in her dreamy voice, "Such strange creatures haunt us, don't they?"

"What?" I asked, turning to her. She gazed out at the patchy snow that showed on the ground beneath the trees and dusted the pine needles.

"What's that, dear?" she asked.

"What strange creatures haunt you?" I asked, my heart pounding. Maybe we weren't crazy. Maybe she had some kind of premonitions, an ability she'd passed down to me.

"Did I say that?" she asked.

"Gramma," I said, setting down my cup and taking her hand in mine. "Do you ever see anything in these woods? Or hear things. Anything... Out of place?"

She smiled at me over the rim of her coffee cup. "Who's to say what is out of place and what belongs?" she asked, her eyes twinkling with mischief.

I sighed, frustrated with her cryptic answer. "I just want to know the truth."

"The truth is more complicated than we know," she said. "What is the truth, anyway? What you can see? What you have seen? What you haven't seen but know in your bones to be true?"

I blinked at her, surprised at her lucidity. I'd thought she was going off on one of her daydreams. "I guess it's all that," I said.

"Then you have your answer," she said. "Let's have dinner, shall we?"

After dinner, when I heard the wolves in the woods, I sat listening for a minute and then laced up my boots. I'd left well enough alone for a while, but it hadn't stopped my nightmares, hadn't stopped me from wondering every moment of every day, what was real and what wasn't. Was I crazy after all? Was it more crazy to believe the impossible things I'd seen or to deny them even though I had a shredded jacket and a hundred strange instances to back me up?

I left a note on the counter and slipped out the back door, pulling my new jacket around me. My breath fogged the cold air in front of me as I stepped off the back porch and onto the grass. My boots crunched softly as I crossed the grass. For a long minute, I stood at the edge of the woods, staring into the darkness. The moon was high and full overhead, so bright that I needed no flashlight in the open spaces. But the shadows under the pines held secrets that seemed to shift and sigh as I waited.

When nothing happened, I started into the woods. If I wanted answers, I was going to have to hunt them down. I was ready.

As I walked, the fear melted away, replaced with determination and certainty. I was going to find my wolf. If he wasn't going to leave me alone, why should I leave him alone? There must be some reason I had been dreaming about him all these years. I let the distant howls guide me, drawing me deeper and deeper into the forest.

At last, the howl that sounded was so close I could almost feel it as well as hear it. The sound pressed into me, raising the hairs on the back of my neck and sending shivers through my body. Still, I went forward as if drawn by an invisible force, my boots crunching in a patch of snow. I stepped out into a clearing and stopped, my breath coming out in a plume of fog when I saw a pair of eyes shining out of the darkness at me. Then I saw another, and another, and another, until six pairs of eyes surrounded me. I swallowed hard, my heart beating like hummingbird wings inside me.

A wolf stepped out of the trees, stalking toward me. Before it could make it more than a few steps, another one stepped out and pushed in front of the first. Somehow, I knew this was my wolf. My heart stilled, and I took a deep breath, waiting for what came next.

Two more wolves slunk from the shadows, but my wolf stood his ground, turning and letting out a long, low growl. He touched his nose to another wolf's and then another. This one stared at him, and for a long minute, they didn't move. I balled my hands into fists, sending a silent plea into the night. At last, one by one, the wolves turned and trotted back into the woods until only one remained. He turned, staring at me in the clearing where the moonlight filtered down and the trees stood tall and still as sentinels witnessing this moment.

"I'm not crazy," I whispered. "It's not a dream."

The wolf stepped forward, crossing the pine needles on silent feet. It stopped in front of me and lifted its muzzle to study me. My knees gave way, and I dropped in front of the wolf, burying my hands in its thick, warm ruff. I stared into his eyes, aching for him to speak to me even though I knew he couldn't. He'd told me enough. It was real. I was touching him. He wasn't just a dream, wasn't just a hallucination. I ran my hands down his sleek, powerful shoulders and down his front legs, then dug them deep into his ruff again.

"It's you," I said. Somehow, I knew. Impossible as it was, I knew. He'd told me it was a dream, but it wasn't. "I know it's you," I said. "I've known all along, I think, in some way. I've known you since I was a kid. I've been dreaming about you for years. How could I not know you when I saw you, that first day outside the school? Part of me always knew, Alarick. I tried to believe it wasn't real, tried to believe you, but I can't."

Suddenly, he twisted away, turning his back and lowering his head. His body began to shake violently, twisting and contorting to unnatural angles. After a minute, he turned back, and even though I'd known, seeing it still made me gasp and take a step back, nearly crying out. It was really him.

Alarick stood before me in the flesh—in human form. I swallowed, backing away a step, but he was faster. He seized me by the shoulders, his eyes flashing. "What do you know?" he demanded. "What have you seen?"

"Nothing," I said automatically, still too stunned by what I'd seen—the transformation not only from wolf to man but from a silent, animal that let me run my hands along his muzzle and around his ears to a human with rough hands and fury blazing in his eyes.

"You said you dreamed about us," he said. "What did you see? How did you know about us?"

"I just knew," I said. "But I don't know anything else. I just know who you are. It's not like I'm spying on you."

"Then what's it like?" he asked, his grip loosening as his eyes became more wary than angry.

I opened my mouth, and again I found myself pouring it all out to him. How the dreams were so real I couldn't tell them from reality, how I couldn't tell reality from dreams since I got here, and how I thought I was losing my mind.

"And I don't know what happened that night you found me," I said. "Maybe I was sleepwalking. Maybe I really did kidnap Brooklyn and Nancy. Maybe I hurt them. I thought it was you, but Brooklyn likes you. She hates me. Did I lure her out into the woods somehow? And Nancy?"

"No," Alarick said, glancing over his shoulder as a wolf howled further off. "You didn't hurt anyone. But you need to go."

"No," I burst out, grabbing his arm. Only then did I fully realize he wasn't wearing anything. His skin was cool to the touch, smooth and soft under my fingers. The moonlight played off the ridges of muscle in his shoulders, his broad chest and chiseled abs, down to the V-shape leading my eyes from his hipbones downward…

I tore my eyes up, back to his face. To my surprise, he wasn't smirking at me for once. His eyes smoldered with the same longing I felt. My breath caught as he stepped forward. The next second, his hand slipped behind me, and his mouth crashed into mine. I was so startled that I didn't realize I was kissing him back for a second. My body reacted instinctually, as if it had been made for this. My hands slid around his neck, burrowing into his thick blond hair the same way they'd sank into his ruff. My body swayed against his, my back arching to get closer, to press against him.

A low growl started in his throat, but he didn't pull away. His lips ravaged mine as his hand slid behind my neck, cradling my head and drawing my chin up as he stooped to meld his lips with mine. His other hand caught my waist, drawing me closer, against the animal heat radiating from his body. I let out a gasp against his mouth, and he took my parted lips for an invitation. His tongue dipped between my lips, meeting mine and caressing it in a way that made every part of me melt. I swooned against him, trying not to moan aloud with pleasure. His hand tightened on my hip, drawing me even tighter against him. I didn't know how this had happened. We'd never done anything but fight, but suddenly, this seemed so natural, so obvious, I didn't know how we hadn't been doing it all along.

A howl sounded in the woods, barely registering with me until Alarick yanked back. His eyes were blazing, a mixture of desire and panic clouding his gaze.

"Go home," he said through shallow breaths.

"I know what you are," I said. "I know for sure. I've seen it. Let me be part of this."

Alarick shook his head. "No. It's not safe for you. You shouldn't know this much. I wasn't supposed to show you. Now…"

"Now I know," I said again. "There's no use in hiding. Don't you want to know why I dreamed about you?"

"Yes," Alarick said begrudgingly. "But I can't. Just go, Timberlyn."

I shook my head, my throat tightening. After that kiss, he was just going to disappear and act like nothing had happened?

"But it has to mean something," I blurted, not sure if I was talking about the dreams or the kiss.

"It doesn't matter," he said. He stepped closer, a sadness coming into his eyes as he took my hand. "You can't be here. You can't be part of this. Just go back to your grandmother's, where you're safe. This will be nothing but another one of your dreams."

"But why?" I asked, aware of how pathetic I sounded but unable to stop myself. I had to have the answer. I'd come out here to find the truth. I had to have it.

"I can't protect you," he said, tensing as another howl sounded, this one closer. "That's all I was ever trying to do. To keep you from going to Ravenwood, from us, from this forest. You have to get out of here now, before it's too late. Go, Timberlyn, and never tell anyone about this."

"Protect me from what?" I asked, throwing my hands up in frustration. "What's going on, Alarick?"

In answer, he stepped back from me and dropped to all fours. I bit back tears, finally swiping away the few that spilled. When Alarick lifted his head, he was a wolf again. His lips drew back to bare a row of razor-sharp fangs, and he let out a menacing growl.

So that was it. That was why we couldn't be part of each other's lives. He was the monster, and I was the girl who drew them. I'd come out here seeking the truth, and I'd found it. But the truth didn't set me free. It broke my heart.

Chapter Seventeen

For the next few weeks, I walked around in a sort of trance. Alarick wasn't just a Wolf, he was a *wolf.* I was pretty sure that they all were. It was so impossible that I had a hard time wrapping my brain around it, and yet, it was the only possibility.

When I saw him in the hall, a jolt went through me, so intense I nearly doubled over. I stumbled over my own feet, the ache in my chest overwhelming me, choking me.

"You okay?" Svana asked, her pretty purple eyes going wide as she stared at me. And then she looked up, following my gaze.

I should have been stealthy, looked away, pretended it wasn't him. But I couldn't pretend. I couldn't look away, even as his eyes swept over me with such cold indifference that it stopped my heart in my chest.

"Oh my god," Svana said, rolling her eyes and grabbing my arm. She dragged me down the hall and into the bathroom, pushing the door closed behind her. Turning to me, she planted her hands on the gentle curve of her narrow hips. "Spill."

I shook my head. "You'll hate me," I said. "You hate them. It's nothing, anyway."

"That wasn't nothing," she protested. "Am I or am I not your best friend?"

"You are," I said, slumping against the wall.

"Best friend code dictates you tell me every last detail," she said with a grin. "You and Alarick Wolf? King of the jungle? Lord of the beasts? How did that happen?"

"It's not what you're thinking," I said. I didn't know what it was, so I didn't elaborate.

"Is that why you've been so weird all week? He broke your heart? Because we can make him sorry.

What'd he do? Leave before you woke up? Girl, I warned you." She shook her head, but her eyes held only sympathy.

"We didn't hook up," I said. "I told you, it wasn't like that."

"Well, if you didn't hook up, that's a first for him," she said. "Or so I hear."

"I'm fine," I said. "Really. Besides, what are you going to do to him? You said it yourself—it's better to not get involved."

"Well, I wasn't going to beat him up," she said, a sly smile starting on her lips. "But there are other ways to make a boy sorry he dropped you too soon."

"Like what?" I had no plans to do anything to Alarick. I just wanted to know what she had in mind.

"Like looking fabulous and going to a party with me this weekend instead of staying home making cookies with your grandma."

"I like doing that," I protested. "Plus, I'm supposed to keep an eye on her."

"You haven't come out with us all year," Svana said. "It's Valentines weekend. Can't she spare you for one evening?"

"Maybe," I muttered. The truth was, I did want to go out once in a while. But I also wanted to watch the woods behind Gramma's house, to see if I could spot the wolves. Somehow, I was tied to them. I wanted to know why I'd dreamed of them. I wanted to know if the other monsters in my dreams were real, too. Maybe I had accepted it so readily because I'd always known in some way that the dreams meant something. Maybe even those middle school mean girls had somehow sensed that the dreams weren't just dreams, and that's why they'd ostracized me.

"Yay!" Svana said, clapping her long, delicate hands together like I'd already agreed. She linked her arm through mine and marched me out of the bathroom. The bell tolled, and we hurried to our classes. When I slid into my seat in science, I didn't glance back at Adolf and Brooklyn, but I could feel them there.

And I was tired of it. I was tired to trying to figure them out. Tired of being shoved aside, ignored, excluded. If they didn't want me in their lives, fine. Svana was right. I was better off just leaving them alone. I'd go out with her and Viktor, have a normal weekend. I had come here to escape the teasing, but also to escape being an outcast. In some weird way, I'd fallen back into the role even though no one had assigned it to me.

I was still drawing monsters. Obsessing about them. Worrying about my dreams. Going to Gramma's instead of parties so I could watch the woods for my wolves.

But Alarick had made it clear that the fascination was not mutual. That we were too different to be part of each other's worlds. So, I'd go be part of Svana's. I'd go do normal things, the ones I hadn't been invited to back home. The things my parents thought I was doing, the things I'd wanted to do. I needed to break free of the weird hold the wolves and their secret had on me and do something fun for a change.

That weekend, I went home to Gramma's, made sure everything was going well, and tidied up the house before asking if I could go out on Saturday.

"Of course, Marla," she said, patting my cheek and smiling. "You don't have to ask."

My throat tightened the way it did every time she called me by Mom's name. "No, forget it," I said. "I don't have to go. It's no big deal."

"Well, of course it is," Gramma said. "You should go out with your friends while you can."

A shiver worked its way down my spine. "What do you mean, while I can?"

"While you're young, of course," she said. "It only happens once, as they say."

After reassuring me a few more times that she'd be okay and that she was by herself all week and did just fine, Gramma had me convinced. I headed to my room to call Svana, who arrived half an hour later with Viktor in tow. He was carrying an oversized duffle and looked distinctly out of his element.

"Who's this one?" Gramma asked, her eyes twinkling as she surveyed Viktor from head to toe.

"This is my friend Viktor," I said.

"A friend, eh?" Gramma said with a Cheshire grin. "Well, it never hurts to keep a friend like that on the back burner."

"Gramma," I scolded, embarrassment flooding me.

"Oh, don't mind me," she said, waving a hand at us. "Go get changed for this party. And don't forget to show me what you're wearing before you leave, so I can be scandalized."

"Sorry," I muttered to Viktor as I hurried my friends down the hall.

"I like her," Svana said. "She's feisty. Now I know where you get it."

"I have no idea what you're talking about," I said, sticking up my nose and surveying the closet.

"Oh, no, you don't," Svana said, grabbing my arm and steering me to the bed, where Viktor had set the duffle. "No more black. Tonight, I get to dress you."

"Oh god, you sound like my parents," I said through a laugh. But Svana could not be swayed, and by the time she was halfway through the makeover, I was having as much fun as she was. Getting a makeover from a friend was one of those rites of passage I'd never gotten to experience, and once I was standing in front of the mirror, even I was impressed. I wasn't bad looking, I just didn't spend a lot of time on my appearance on the average day. But tonight, I had more than my old standby, mascara and gloss.

Tonight, my lips looked pink and pouty, contrasting with the rest of my smoky-eyed, sophisticated makeup. My usually straight hair lay in loose waves across my shoulders, and a sexy red minidress hugged my curves.

"Two words," Svana said, standing back and looking me up and down. "Bomb. Shell."

"I think that's one word," I said, laughing and smoothing my hands self-consciously over the dress. I didn't wear dresses. Before tonight, the closest I'd come was my school uniform. But I felt too good to take it off.

For once, I didn't want to hide behind black and disappear. I wanted to stand out.

"Viktor's going to bust a nut when he sees you," she said.

"What? Why?"

"Come on, Timberlyn," she said, rolling her eyes. "You can't be that naïve. You must know my brother has a thing for you."

"He does?" I asked, my heart doing something funny in my chest. At one point, it had crossed my mind. He was undeniably gorgeous, and there was always an awkward moment when we parted. But I'd been so caught up in the wolf stuff for so long that I'd barely paid attention to what was going on in the rest of the school.

Svana just shook her head, threw open the door, and waltzed me into the living room with all the dramatics she possessed. Viktor's eyes bulged, and his Adam's apple bobbed as he swallowed. "Wow," he said, standing from his seat on the couch.

"You can say that again," Gramma said.

"You look… Nice," Viktor said. "Really pretty."

Svana threw her head back and belted out one of those big laughs. "Okay, Romeo," she said. "Let's get going. It was nice to meet you, Gramma. Now that I've met you, I guess I'll give Timberlyn a break for wanting to hang out with you all the time."

I threw an elbow into her ribs, but she only laughed again. We headed out, climbing into a sleek black Audi that waited outside. At Ravenwood, we all wore the same clothes, and I never saw anyone's cars, so I hadn't realized my friends might have quite a bit more money than my family.

"My turn to say *wow*," I said as Viktor held open the passenger door for me. "This is nice."

I felt an all-too-familiar prickle on the back of my neck, and I knew that the wolves were close by. Were they watching us right now? Did they think this was a date?

Then I remembered that I didn't care what they thought. They didn't want me around, and Viktor did. If he wanted to open my door for me, and have me sit in the front next to him like this was a date, what did Alarick care? He'd kissed me that night, but he hadn't even talked to me since then. If anything, he'd been even frostier than before. I didn't see him volunteering to take me out on Valentines.

"Eat your heart out, Alarick Wolf," Svana sang, swinging into the back seat. I was once again reminded how absolutely clumsy I looked next to her. Every move she made was like dancing. Had Alarick seen her get into the car after watching me fumble my way in, trying not to flash Viktor in my short skirt, and sitting there awkwardly while he closed the door? I wondered if they all noticed how plain I was compared to her. But then I thought how silly that was. It didn't matter. She didn't like any of the guys I might be interested in. She hated the Wolf boys, and Viktor was her brother. And even if we liked the same boy at some point, I knew that neither of us would risk our friendship for a boy.

I smiled at my reflection in the window as we pulled out onto the two-lane road. I couldn't see anything in the forest, but I knew they were out there. Watching.

"Where are we going?" I asked, turning away from them.

"There's this all-ages club downtown," Svana said. "You can't drink, but that's not what we're going for anyway."

I scratched my head. "What are we going for?"

"Dancing, of course," she said. "Hanging out. Forgetting certain assholes who aren't worth your time."

I snuck a glance at Viktor, who frowned out the windshield and pushed the car a little faster. It hugged the road, zipping around curves with ease, the engine purring like a kitten.

"Already forgotten," I said.

Svana laughed. "Good. And it'll be cool for you to show up. Everyone's going. They'll be glad to see you hanging out."

My heart skipped. "Everyone?"

Viktor glanced at me. "Not everyone. But a lot of people go there on the weekends."

Svana hadn't exactly said it outright, but I could read between the lines. People thought I was a snob, or strange, or suspicious because I didn't go out with them after school. They were already wary of newcomers, and with the girls disappearing right after I arrived, some people were still uneasy around me even after Brooklyn's return. Who knew what Delilah had told them about me on top of that.

It was time to put all that behind me, though. Time to forget wolves of every sort and be a normal girl.

Whatever that was.

Chapter Eighteen

When we pulled up to the club, it didn't look like much from the outside. But inside, there were two sets of stairs, one leading up and one leading down.

"Amy just texted," Svana said. "Let's go find her."

I was surprised for only a second. When I'd started at Ravenwood, I'd immediately pegged Amy, Brooklyn, and Nancy as among the more superficial girls at the school, the ones who would have been cheerleaders and mean girls at PHS. They were popular. They obviously spent hours on their appearance every morning, not just when they were going out.

But there I was, judging them the way people had always judged me. The way I'd moved to another country to avoid.

Things had changed for Brooklyn, of course, but Amy was the same. She wasn't mean, though. She was the nicest person I'd met aside from Svana and Viktor. We sat together in science and gossiped and helped each other study. She'd never treated me as anything other than a friend, despite our differences of opinion on the Wolf boys. And I knew she and Svana were friendly, so it wasn't a surprise that they hung out here on weekends. After all, Svana was the most beautiful girl in school. Why wouldn't she be popular?

It was harder to tell when we were at school, in classes, and wearing the same clothes. Here, I could tell who was popular more than I ever had at school.

"Svana," Amy squealed as we arrived in the room on the ground floor, where people of all ages were playing pool, darts, shuffleboard, foosball, and vintage arcade games. Amy ran over, wobbling slightly on a pair of sky-high heels, and threw her arms around Svana.

"Did you bring the others?" Svana asked, though it was obvious Amy had brought all her friends. They were all draped over stools and leaning against the wall like a collection of expensive silks, each one in a skirt that barely covered the apex of her thighs and heels that rivaled Amy's. I was wearing Svana's dress, which would have been that short on her, but since I was significantly shorter, it hit a bit lower on my thighs. Still, I marveled at how seamlessly I blended in. Suddenly a strange thought hit me. Was I becoming popular?

"Everyone's already here," Amy said. "And I see you brought the new girl, and ooh, a delicious treat." She squeezed Viktor's arm, and he smiled down at her. I searched for jealousy inside me, but I couldn't tell if I was feeling that or nervousness about the whole night.

Amy laughed at Viktor's expression before throwing her arms around me. I tensed in surprise before returning the embrace. "Hey, Amy."

"You came," she crowed. "I'm so glad. How's your grandma? Svana said you have to take care of her on weekends."

"She's good," I said, shooting Svana a look.

"That's so sweet of you," Amy said, squeezing my arm. "I knew I liked you. I mean, I love my grandma, but I don't know if I'd give up this for her. Not every weekend. How do you ever get laid?"

"Um."

"I'm kidding," she shrieked, slapping my shoulder.

"She's not kidding," Svana said, rolling her eyes.

"Fine, I'm really not," Amy said. "Now, let's go dance so we can find the night's sweet meat."

"Oh my god," I said, laughing. "Is that really what you call your hookups?"

"I could call them hot meat if it makes you feel better," Amy said.

"No, no," I said, holding up both hands. "Call them whatever you want. Not my business."

"Aww, you're still so sweet and innocent," she said as we made our way downstairs. Club music thumped from behind a door at the bottom. "I remember being fifteen."

"You can't be that much older."

"A whole year," she said dramatically. "But I'm new here this year, just like you."

"I didn't know that," I said, half my words cut off when Svana threw open the door, spilling the music around us.

"Yeah," Amy yelled into my ear. "That's why me and Brooklyn and Nancy and the other girls who started with us are all friends. Plus, we have all the same classes."

I was in those classes, too. The thought gave me a shiver.

"You think we're next?" Amy yelled, as if she'd read my mind.

"No, of course not," I said, forcing a laugh.

"I do," Amy said. "That's why I'm having all the fun I can while I'm still around. Plus, I came from a Catholic family. Your Southern upbringing's got nothing on mine. Once I realized what they'd been hiding from me all these years? I'm making up for lost time, girl."

With that, she spun away into the crowd of dancers, latched onto a guy, and started grinding on him with no shame.

"Wow," I said.

Svana threw her head back and laughed. "I told you it was fun," she said when she recovered. "Let's dance. Don't worry, I'll keep all the oldies off you."

Looking around, I saw a lot of guys older than us, mostly college-age, but a few who looked as old as thirty, looking desperate in their trucker hats and skinny jeans. Svana pulled me onto the dance floor. At first, I felt self-conscious with so much skin showing, my bare legs brushing against other dancers. But that was quickly replaced by a swell of joy as my body moved to the music. I didn't know how to dance, but Svana moved with such ridiculous amounts of sexiness and grace that I didn't even try to keep up with her. I just let the beat take over. It felt good to move, to let off steam from the tension of so many weeks of worrying.

Amy and her friends were all dancing with us, some with guys and some without. Most of them didn't seem to care what they looked like dancing, either. This was my chance to prove that I was just like them. That I wanted to be part of the social scene, that I could be fun and let loose like they did on the weekend. To act like I wasn't different and that I didn't have secrets. What would they do if they knew what I did? If they knew the Wolf boys were a million times more dangerous than they'd ever imagined, that they were freaks a thousand times more unnatural than me?

I could just imagine Svana's gleeful joy in hearing such a thing, in getting a chance to take them down. I could imagine Amy's shrieks of horror when she found out she'd slept with a monster. But I knew what it was like to be the freak, the monster, and I couldn't do that to the Wolf boys. Not even for my friends.

The Wolf posse was already outcast enough, even if they were a different kind of outcast. They might have chosen it themselves, knowing they'd avoid the worst of it if they were above it. But they didn't get to come out and have fun like this. They ran in the woods, hunting. And when they ran across someone…

Now that I'd had time to think, I was sure I had figured it out. Brooklyn had wandered into their woods for some reason, and they'd found her and… Changed her. Now she was like them. Was I supposed to be like them, too? A tiny part of me was jealous. She got to be a part of their lives. She'd even switched classes so that she was in a class with at least one them every period of the day. They'd taken Brooklyn in.

When I'd wandered into the woods, they'd warned me to go back. Did it have to do with when they hunted, or the moon cycle, or something else entirely?

A pair of hands slid around my waist, and I started to pull away, but when I twisted around, I saw Viktor. He gave me a questioning look, and I smiled up at him. I wasn't here to think about the Wolf boys. I was here to have fun, to dance with a boy who might even like me.

We danced for a song, and then another, and then another. Time disappeared, and I let my mind stop moving for once, focusing only on the rhythm of the music and my body. After a long time, Svana appeared beside us and yelled that we should go get a drink. I didn't know how long it had been, just that I was hot and tired. Svana's hair was a bit mussed for once, but despite having been dancing for what must have been an hour, I didn't see a drop of sweat on her.

She tugged us to the bar, where we squeezed in beside a big man with a crew cut who was sitting on a barstool facing away from the bar while a girl I vaguely recognized from school was straddling his lap, gyrating to the music. I turned away, trying not to stare though the guy must have been around forty and wearing a business suit. To each their own.

"What do you want?" Svana yelled to me. "I have an ID if you want a real drink." She grinned and wiggled her eyebrows, but I shook my head and asked for a Coke.

"Hey, Ginger," barked a deep voice that cut under the music. I glanced over to see the big guy leering at my body, and for the first time all night, I saw the other side of wearing clothes like this. They didn't just make me feel confident. They drew unwanted attention.

"There's only one reason a girl wears a dress like that," the guy said as the girl on his lap began to bounce up and down in a frantic rhythm, her skirt pushed up so far that I could see her underwear.

"Looks like you've got your hands full to me," I said, turning away. Svana was leaning over the bar trying to flag down the bartender, so I smiled at Viktor, hoping he'd see the plea in my eyes. Maybe only girls got that silent communication style, though, because he just smiled and turned to order his drink.

"I got two hands," the creepy guy said. "So tell me why'd you wear that dress if you weren't planning for a guy like me to take it off."

Damn it, he wasn't going to quit. I summoned some of the bitchiness I'd used to survive at home and turned to him with my best go-to-hell look.

"Maybe I just like it," I said.

"Me, too," he said. "But I'd like it better on my floor."

"In case you hadn't noticed, half the girls in here are wearing less than this. You think they all want to get with some old guy?"

"Maybe they do," he said.

"Well, good for them," I said. "It's really none of my business what they do. But I'm not interested."

Suddenly the crowd parted, and Alarick was standing in front of us, his brows lowered and a thunderous expression in his dark eyes. "Time to go."

I was too stunned to respond, but the older guy turned to me with a leering smile. "So, you're the girl causing my sons all this trouble." His eyes roved over my curves. "If you're making it worth their while, I can see why they put up with you."

My mind was reeling. For a second, I'd thought Alarick was talking to me. But he hadn't even spared me a sideways glance. He was talking to the sleazebag next to me. This creep was Mr. Wolf, the guy who owned half the town and the school.

"Let's go," Alarick growled at his father. He grabbed the girl off Mr. Wolf's lap and set her on her feet. She gave a yelp of protest and glared at Alarick, but he didn't see it. His eyes were fixed on his father with such rage that it made me shrink back on my seat.

"Coming," Mr. Wolf said, with a bright, false smile. "Just make sure I get a turn with the ginger when you pass her around."

Alarick grabbed his father and hauled him off the chair. His father was big, but Alarick was bigger, and his body bulged with muscles while Mr. Wolf looked like a body builder who had begun to eat more than he worked out. He was a bit soft in the middle, his face becoming jowly. But when he gripped Alarick's arms, I could see his thick muscles bunching. His face had gone red as he strained against his son. They stood locked together for a minute, gripping each other like two boxers trying to decide where to land a punch. People had gone quiet around them, turning to watch.

But instead of throwing a punch, Mr. Wolf finally flung himself away from Alarick and stormed out, Alarick following. They disappeared in seconds, leaving me wondering what the hell that was about, and thinking it was no surprise the Wolf boys were such assholes if that was their dad. And some small part of me ached that Alarick hadn't even spared me a single look, despite what Svana had said about the dress. He'd looked through me like I was nothing, like I was no more important than the girl he'd pried off his father's lap.

But I knew that I was. Even if I meant as little to him, even if he couldn't feel the connection, I could. I knew without a doubt that I was meant to play some part in their lives. If only they'd stop pushing me away long enough for me to figure out what I was supposed to do.

"Earth to Timberlyn," Svana shouted, pushing my shoulder playfully. "Your ice is melting."

"Sorry," I said.

"What did Mr. Wolf say to you?" she asked, a teasing smile on her lips. "Did he invite you to work at his strip club?"

"Surprisingly, no."

Svana threw back her head and laughed. She was holding a glass of what looked like red wine. "I bet Alarick almost died when he saw you in that dress."

I decided to avoid that topic altogether. "I thought you didn't come here to drink."

"I said it's not why I come here," she said with a grin. "I didn't say I don't enjoy a drink on occasion."

Amy came running up to the bar, and I was relieved to see I wasn't the only one with damp hair and a flushed face from the dancing. "I'm dying for a drink," she said. "Sip?"

"Drink hers," Svana said, pointing to my soda.

"You don't mind, do you?" Amy asked, grabbing my soda before giving me a pleading smile. Even though I was thirsty, the Coke was watery now, anyway, so I shrugged and watched her slurp down the entire contents.

"Oh my god, this is my favorite song," Amy shrieked, throwing her arms above her head and shimmying her hips. "Viktor, come dance with me."

"Want to go back out?" Svana asked when Amy had grabbed Viktor's hand and dragged him to the dance floor.

"I'm going to sit here a minute," I said. "I need another drink anyway. You go. Have fun."

"You're not going to pout about Alarick all night, are you?" she asked, a frown creasing her pretty brow.

"I'm fine," I said. But I wasn't sure. I got a soda and sat there sipping it until they came back a while later. Even dancing had lost its appeal, though. My mind couldn't let go this time, couldn't go with the music and lose all thought. By the time Viktor dropped me off at Gramma's later, I was sure I'd annoyed my friends with my moodiness.

I lay in bed for a while, but I couldn't sleep. I had to see the wolves. My wolf.

I wouldn't think his name. I didn't care about the boy. I cared about the animal, the one I'd dreamed of for so long that he seemed a part of me.

I climbed out of bed and dressed as if in a trance. This time, my only fear as I stepped into the forest was that I wouldn't find them. My boots squelched in the wet pine needles as I headed deeper into the forest. No wolf howls echoed through the woods tonight, and the moon didn't let nearly enough light through the canopy of pine needles. I walked for a long time, not sure where I was going. I was so tired I couldn't think, couldn't remember where I'd come from or where I'd already been. I wasn't scared of getting lost, though. Either I'd find my way, or Alarick would find me.

The slightest hint of morning light had just come into the sky when I found a path. It wasn't well worn, and

I could just make it out in the scant light. I followed it without hesitation, sure it would lead me to the wolves, to their gathering place.

Instead, I came out a few minutes later in a tiny clearing with a worn, wooden shack in the middle. My heart began to thunder in my ears as I crept forward. When I reached the door, I found a padlock on the outside. Alarick had said his father hunted in these woods. Did that mean he was a wolf like his sons? If not, did he know what they were? Was this a regular hunting cabin, or something more?

I tugged at the lock to make sure it was latched, then went to the lone window. It was grimy, and when I pressed my face to it, I could see only shadows within. Damn it. I hadn't brought a flashlight, but I was wide awake now.

And then I heard something that made my blood freeze. Somewhere in the woods, I heard a scream.

It wasn't a wolf. It was a human scream.

Heart stampeding in my chest, I jumped away from the cabin and ran. I tore through the trees, not sure if I was trying to find the person who had screamed or find my way home and hide under the blankets, believing it was all in my head. I ran until my breath was gone, and all I had were little gasps that ripped from my lungs with painful heat. A cramp gripped my side, but I ran through it. I ran without even trying to keep track of where I was, my internal compass long forgotten. Until my only thought was escape. At last, I saw light ahead, the end of this dark, nightmare forest. I stumbled out of the woods onto manicured lawn of Ravenwood Academy, with a few wisps of mist lying over the greens like the picturesque campus it wanted us to believe it was.

Did they know what the Wolf boys were? Did they know what they'd done to Brooklyn? And what about Nancy? Why hadn't she come back? Had she refused even more forcefully than Brooklyn? From the way she acted, it didn't seem like Brooklyn had changed willingly. And yet, I wandered into the woods, asking for it, and they'd done nothing to me.

I didn't really want to be a wolf, not like they were. Not like Brooklyn was. She never spoke anymore, and people shied away from her. They stared at her when she walked down the hall with the five boys. They moved aside to let her pass, just as they did with the boys. Plus, she didn't seem to care about herself anymore. Her hair was always uncombed and usually unwashed. If someone did speak to her—even a teacher—she'd snarl at them to leave her alone. It didn't look like a happy life.

But as much as I'd tried to forget it, I couldn't. How could people be wolves? And why did I dream of them, and Lindy, and other things I'd never seen before? Maybe those monsters were out there, too. I had to know. To find out, at long last, the answers I'd been seeking all along.

No answers came to me that day, but on Monday morning when I walked the halls of Ravenwood, the familiar whispers made my stomach clench with dread.

"…didn't come home…"

"…hasn't heard from her…"

"…third girl…"

My whole body was shaking by the time I found Svana at her locker, a grim expression on her pretty face.

"Tell me it's not what I think," I said. "Another girl disappeared? When?"

"Saturday night," she said, grimacing as she shoved a book in her locker.

"This is ridiculous," I burst out. "How can the school not do something about it? They should shut down classes."

"It didn't happen on campus," she said. "None of them did, as far as we know. The school can't do anything about it except cooperate with the investigation."

"Who was it this time?" I asked, thinking of the girl I'd seen riding Mr. Wolf's lap.

Svana slammed her locker and turned to me. "It was Amy."

Chapter Nineteen

We stared at each other for a minute, the shock knocking the heat off my anger, turning my stomach sour and cold. Not that she was any more important than the other girls, but I knew Amy. I had only seen Brooklyn once before she'd disappeared, and though I had lots of classes with Nancy, we hadn't talked. But Amy? How could someone so bursting with life, laughter, and loudness… How could she just vanish? How could someone silence that volume of living?

And then I remembered the scream in the woods.

A shiver went through me, and I pulled Svana to my locker, opening the door so I could whisper behind it. I didn't want to risk a Wolf walking by and overhearing or reading my lips or whatever they could do.

"I saw a shack in the woods," I said. "I was hiking around there on Saturday. The door was locked, but I'm going back. I'm sure I can find my way back. I'm going to break in. There might be some clues there, or…"

"It's on *their* property," she whispered, her eyes solemn.

"I heard a scream in the woods," I hissed. "If there's even a chance they put Amy there, that we could get her back, we have to go."

"You can't go on their property, Timberlyn. You met Mr. Wolf."

I remembered Alarick's words about anything on their property being theirs. And I remembered how much Amy wanted another chance with Adolf. Had she wanted it enough that she'd go into the woods with him?

Yeah. She definitely had.

Maybe I was playing with fire. But I hadn't been burned yet. And I wasn't just going to look the other way while they took Amy and turned her into a bitter zombie like Brooklyn.

"You can go with me or not," I said. "But I'm going back."

A low voice cut in. "I'll go."

I jerked back from my locker, startled. Viktor stood behind me, his face as solemn as his sister's.

"You can't," Svana said. "They'll kill you."

"You want me to let them kill Timberlyn?" he asked, his eyes steady on Svana. And even though I was sure they wouldn't really kill me, Viktor's expression was dead serious.

"You guys are crazy," Svana said. "You can't go tromping through the woods, especially ones that belong to Mr. Wolf."

"And I can't just sit here and do nothing about Amy," I shot back.

Svana's jaw tensed, and she glared at her brother for a second. "Fine," she snapped at last. "It's your funeral."

She turned and left in a huff.

"You didn't have to do that," I said. "You don't have to go."

"I can't let you go alone," he said, giving me a little smile. "It wouldn't be safe."

A little flutter started in my belly as he held my gaze, leaning in a tiny fraction. I'd never felt that way from Viktor's presence before, and I wasn't sure what to think of it now. I didn't have time to dwell on it, though, because the familiar hush fell in the hall, and the hairs prickled along my spine.

I didn't look away from Viktor, though. I stood rooted to the spot, my heartbeat quickening as the posse approached. Instead of sweeping by this time, they stopped. The hallway seemed to take a collective inhalation.

"Get lost, Egilsson," Adolf said, throwing out a hand and shoving Viktor's shoulder. Viktor crashed into the locker. He rebounded, holding his shoulder and glaring at the other boy. His tall, lean body looked tensed and coiled to strike like a snake.

"Leave him alone," I said, stepping between them.

Adolf ignored me and spoke to Viktor over my head. "Leave *her* alone."

"Um, not your place," I snapped, planting my hands on my hips. "Viktor's my friend."

"I need to talk to you," Alarick said, glaring at Viktor. "Without him."

I shook my hair back, resisting the urge to say something petty about him deciding to speak to me again now that another guy was showing interest. So predictable.

"Anything you have to say, you can say to me right here," I said instead.

Alarick's jaw worked back and forth, his eyes narrowed at Viktor. When my friend didn't scurry off as the Wolf boys apparently expected, he fixed his gaze on me. "Fine," he said. "Stay away from my family. Since you didn't listen last time, I thought you might need a reminder."

"Since you didn't pick up on it last time, I guess you need a reminder—your threats don't work on me. Sorry."

I could feel the shifting of the crowd in the hall, a murmur rippling down the corridor. I hadn't meant to have a showdown at my locker, but I was sick of this. Especially if he thought he'd use my friends to get to me, to 'remind' me to get in line.

For a second, he didn't react. Despite my unruffled exterior, my heart was thundering in my chest, and I could barely draw a breath. I'd seen this guy stare down his own father, a man much older and almost as big as him. I'd seen what he'd done to Brooklyn. I'd seen what he could turn into, who he really was. A deadly predator who could slice my jugular with one canine, tear my heart out with his teeth.

At last, a strange smile twisted his lips, and he stepped closer and slid his arms around me, securing them at my lower back. Suddenly, I was back in the woods, my back against a pine, his hands in my hair, his mouth on my mouth. My breath deserted me, my whole body painfully alive, aching with his touch.

"Then maybe this will convince you," he purred in my ear. "You want to be my girlfriend? Is that what it'll take to keep you away from my dad?"

The memory of his father's sleazy comments at the bar jolted me back to reality. I shoved myself off Alarick's stone chest, and he released me with a chuckle.

"Seems to me like y'all are the ones who can't leave me alone," I said, hating the quaver in my voice. My head was spinning with the effect he had on me, my blood still thrumming with an unnatural charge, my mind clouded with his pine trees-and-wild wind scent.

He laughed, and his brothers joined in, along with Vance, Jose, and Brooklyn. They were all still laughing when I turned and strode down the hall, fighting tears and rage and the weakness that came over me when he touched me. What was wrong with me? I should hate him and all of them. And yet, this unnatural pull kept me wanting more. I couldn't seem to shake it. Was it just the dreams? I knew him somehow, knew them deeper than what they seemed on the surface. I had seen into them in my dreams, had known them all my life. And after all, they were unnatural. Why shouldn't my attraction to them be the same?

Over the next week, I tried to find a way to get back into the woods, but something always stopped me. Things were tense on campus again. People walked in pairs or even groups, hurrying as if a shadow lurked just behind them. And though no one gave me suspicious looks anymore, I couldn't help but wonder. I'd given Amy my drink. Had that drink been meant for me? Had it been spiked with whatever they'd given me on Halloween to make me forget? Had they meant to take me that night?

I tried to go into the woods that weekend, but the whole pack of them appeared to chase me out, snarling and snapping until I ran back to Gramma's to hide like a coward. But I was just a human. What else could I do? I had no silver bullets.

After that, I stopped trying. Outwardly, I kept my head down and followed the rules, just like all the other students at Ravenwood. I went to my classes and drew pine trees without wolves under them. I ate the delicious food that now tasted like sawdust. I waited for the police to swarm the woods and was not surprised when they didn't. In the hallway, when the Wolf posse passed, I didn't meet their eyes. I hoped they'd believe they'd scared me into giving up. That I wouldn't try again.

But I knew they weren't convinced. Not yet. For the next few weeks, I tried to stay out of the way of the Wolf gang, but they seemed to be everywhere. Donovan walked past my seat in art three or four times a day. Did he really need that many art supplies? Adolf strolled past my seat slowly in science, dropping his pencil beside me or knocking something off my desk as he went. Alarick was in the hall, in my classes, in the cafeteria, always there, though he never spoke to me. The two friends and Brooklyn stared just as much. I felt like I was walking on eggshells, always being watched. Like they were waiting for something.

I wasn't going to give it to them. But I wasn't giving up. Not that easily.

I was waiting, too. Waiting for a full moon, when the light would show me the monsters. Waiting for Viktor to stop making excuses and to come with me. Waiting for an opportunity. And in my mind, I was retracing every single one of the panicked steps I took until I was sure I could find my way to the shack again. Pretty sure, anyway.

I had other things on my mind, too. I had midterms to study for, and spring break, for which I couldn't fly home. After Thanksgiving and Christmas, we couldn't afford another international flight. Instead, I went to Seattle with Svana and Viktor, where we rented a couple hotel rooms with a few other students. And even though I felt a little out of place, and my mind was always elsewhere, I managed to have fun exploring the city, taking the ferry, and visiting the Space Needle.

The whole time, my mind kept going back to Amy. She would have come along on the trip if she could. Actually, she would have been the center of the group, spearheading the trip. I kept thinking how much she would have wanted to go to a club, and how she would have squealed at the fish smell of the harbor.

When we returned to Ravenwood, everything was quiet except my mind. I was done waiting. At the next full moon, I was ready. I didn't know the wolves' patterns exactly, but I knew they hung out in the woods outside Gramma's every full moon. I'd seen them. I didn't know if they were there for me—why would they be? They refused to let me in on whatever was going on. And yet, I didn't know why else they would watch Gramma's house. When I'd asked, she'd admitted to seeing them, but then she'd just said nothing was as it seemed.

I went home to Gramma's the weekend of the full moon in April, but I didn't stay long. Just until the moon started to rise. Then I called Viktor.

A few minutes later, he arrived in his Audi. I was surprised to see Svana in the back seat when I opened the door.

"I thought you weren't down for trespassing," I said, shutting the door and twisting around to see her.

"I'm not," she said with a shrug. "But as your best friend, it's my sworn duty to protect you from bullies, strange men in bars, and even yourself. So, here I am."

I thought about that for the whole ride back to Ravenwood. By the time we reached the academy, I knew I couldn't let them go on this trek with me.

"Y'all, I have to tell you something," I said when we climbed out of the Audi in the special student garage that was tucked away behind the school so they could pretend they didn't need such modern conveniences.

"You're really in love with Alarick Wolf?" Svana guessed. "Because I kinda already figured that one out."

"What? No, I'm not."

"Says the girl who can't see him walk by without hyperventilating," Svana said, rolling her eyes. "I get it, Timberlyn. You're obviously not the first girl to fall into that trap."

I thought of Brooklyn, and Nancy, and Amy. Had they fallen into that trap?

"That's not what this is about," I said, shaking my head. "But I can't in good conscience let you come with me. The Wolf boys are… Different."

"Yeah," Svana said. "We know. They're not like other guys, and you're not like other girls, and they're really super nice under all that psycho-ness."

"No," I said slowly. My heart was hammering, and I suddenly had to steady myself on Viktor's car. "I mean, they're not… Entirely… Human."

Viktor's brows shot up, and he glanced at Svana, who also looked alarmed.

"What do you mean, not entirely human?" she asked, her eyes narrowing. "Like, they're soulless robots, and that's why they're so evil?"

"Like their name is not the only thing that's Wolf."

I looked from one blank face to the other, my heart drumming. Would they believe me?

"What are you talking about?" Viktor asked. "Are you telling us they're… What? *Werewolves*?"

"Well… Yeah," I said, swallowing hard. "I guess that's what you'd call them. I know it sounds crazy, and you probably think I'm as psycho as they are, but I saw it with my own eyes. I saw Alarick… *Change*."

"Um, yeah," Svana said. "That sounds completely crazy, Timberlyn."

"But… Plausible?" I asked hopefully. "I know, I know. It sounds insane even to my own ears. But I'm telling you. I saw them."

Viktor shook his head slowly. "I can't believe I'm having to say this to someone in real life," he said. "But Timberlyn. Come on. There's no such thing as werewolves."

"Yeah," Svana said. "I think maybe your obsession with the Wolf brothers has gone too far. I mean, do you hear yourself right now? Like, I don't think you're lying or anything. I see that you really believe it. I almost want to believe it for you, but…"

But I'm crazy, I thought. Just like everyone back home said all along.

I could see the pity in their eyes, could see that they really wanted to help me, that they really were my friends.

"Don't you think this has gone on long enough?" Viktor asked, placing a gentle hand on my shoulder.

"Don't you think you should maybe... I don't know. Forget about them?"

I looked from one of my friends to the other. My best friends. The best friends I'd ever had in my whole life. Friends who I was now alienating because of my dreams and my obsession with the monsters that lurked therein. I'd made that mistake once, and I'd spent the next few years of my life as an outcast, dreading every day. If I had to pretend to keep that from happening again, I would. I wasn't going to lose my friends a second time.

"Yeah, you're right," I said, forcing a laugh. "I really should forget it. I'm sure it was just a really vivid dream."

I'd said those words once before, in middle school. I'd told someone my dreams. But I hadn't said they were real. This was so much worse. I trusted my friends, but I couldn't expect them to believe the impossible. I could only hope they wouldn't spread rumors around the school, make me the leper I had been at home. I didn't think they would. They were good people, even if they couldn't make this leap of faith. They hadn't seen it. Of course they couldn't believe.

Chapter Twenty

"Timberlyn," Svana said as we walked back toward the dorm. "You're going to find the cabin again, anyway. Aren't you?"

I bit my tongue, wanting to tell her the truth. But I couldn't endanger my friends like that. They didn't know what they were up against. And I couldn't be sure that the Wolf brothers wouldn't hurt them. For some reason, they refused to take me, to hurt me. I didn't know if that would hold true for my friends, though. I probably couldn't stop them from taking more girls, but maybe I could get proof. I had my phone, and all I had to do was take one picture and run back here.

"I won't go back," I said. "You're right. I should just forget it."

My friends were both looking at me like they didn't believe me, and I felt even worse lying to them than I did to my parents. But I had a good reason. A lie to protect someone you cared about, to keep them from being hurt, was excusable. At least I kept telling myself that as we walked across the beautiful, spring-green lawn. I usually didn't stay on campus on weekends, and it was eerily empty as we walked through the twilight, the swollen moon balanced on the horizon.

"Want to hang out?" Svana asked.

"I'll probably just do some drawing," I said.

"Please don't go out there," she said. "You're a girl. You know it's dangerous to walk around at night by yourself. And those guys… They have no morals, Timberlyn. If you really believe they took Amy, you know that."

"Okay," I said, feeling worse every time she made me lie.

She sighed. "Good."

Viktor stood there waiting for us to go inside. But I could feel every minute ticking by. I needed to get there and back tonight, and I didn't know exactly how to find the place. It could take hours. I didn't need another delay.

Svana gave me a quick hug and stood in the second floor hallway while I went to my room. The Wolf posse had been watching me for a month, and now she was monitoring me. I just wanted to be left to do what I had to do. No one else believed me, so I'd just have to do it on my own. The least they could do was let me.

In our room, I found Delilah in her bed, watching something on her laptop. I waited fifteen minutes, but she was clearly not going anywhere. Viktor would have made it back to the boys' dorm by now, and Svana would be in her third-floor room. Which meant it was time to go.

I got up off my bed and started to pull on my boots.

"Where are you going?"

I glanced up at Delilah, her usual sullen expression in place. Maybe she was a werewolf, too. She looked as pissed as Brooklyn all the time, though her grooming habits were much better, and she hated the boys.

"Why do you hate the Wolf brothers so much?" I asked.

"That's where you're going? To hook up with one of them?"

I snorted. "No. I'm going to find Amy and take a picture of her for proof that they're the ones behind the girls disappearing."

Delilah stared at me for a long minute without blinking. Then she threw her blanket off her lap and stood. "I'm in."

My mouth dropped open with shock, and I dropped the laces I'd been tying. "Seriously? Now you want to be friends?"

She pulled open her closet and pulled out a pair of black cargo pants, a black long-sleeved T, and a leather moto vest. "Who said anything about being friends?"

"You've ignored me the entire year," I said, sitting back on my heels. "Now you want to help?"

"I thought you were chasing after the guys," she said from inside her closet as she changed into her black gear. "If someone's ready to take them down, I'm not about to miss it."

She emerged looking like a complete badass punk queen with her short hair and a pair of combat boots on her feet. It struck me then that we probably would have been friends at PHS. She was more goth than I was, and at least twice as angry. A pang of regret went through me that I hadn't tried harder to be her friend. But then, it went both ways. She certainly hadn't taken any steps in that direction.

"You know we're going to be trespassing on Mr. Wolf's property," I clarified. I didn't want anyone walking into this without full understanding, but I didn't know if I could tell her about the Wolf brothers. My friends had already looked at me like I was insane. I knew they were being rational, but the hurt was still fresh. If my friends wouldn't believe me, why would Delilah? I didn't think I could bring myself to open myself up to her kind of scorn.

She rooted around in her nightstand, pulled out a long, black flashlight, and flashed it on and off. "Ready," she said with a vicious gleam in her eye.

I planted my hands on my hips and looked her over. "And you realize we're completely unarmed except for that flashlight."

She smirked as she brushed past me. "Speak for yourself."

"I'm not going in there to hurt anyone," I said, following her down the hall. How had I suddenly become a sidekick on my own mission?

"Always carry protection," she said, starting down the stone staircase toward the bottom floor. "Can't be too careful these days."

"Okay," I said. "I'm just going to get Amy. Not attack someone."

"Oh, don't worry, I won't attack your boyfriend," she said. "But I can't be held responsible for what I might do if someone tries to fuck with me. Self-defense, ya know? All that adrenaline. People have been known to overreact."

"Did anyone ever tell you that you're a little scary?" I asked as I struggled to keep up with her.

"Oh, I'm sorry, were you trying to bring a fluffy bunny for backup?"

We reached the lobby, where the Resident Assistant sat texting. Halfway across the lobby, I glanced over at the same moment she looked up. A scowl darkened her freckled face. "Curfew," she said.

Delilah let out a huff. "Come on, Leigh. I'm just escorting the newbie here to the library."

Leigh, an upperclassman with red-brown hair and an abundance of freckles, shook her head. "You know the rules. You'll just have to go tomorrow."

Delilah sighed and shoved her hands in her pockets. "Well, apparently the rules of Timberlyn's history class are that she has to have sources beyond Wikipedia, and of course she didn't read the fine print until the night before the paper is due."

I wracked my brain for the topic we'd been studying in history, just in case Leigh asked what the paper was on, but she didn't seem all that suspicious. The phone on the desk, an old landline, started ringing. She gave a frustrated sigh. "You guys. With everything that's happened, you shouldn't even want to go out there right now. Just go find something online. I'm sure you can find something besides Wiki."

She snatched up the phone, then gave a growl and replaced the hook when a dial tone sounded. I glanced at Delilah. "We really have to go," I said. "I'm so sorry. You can watch us walk across the common, and the librarian is there, right? We'll ask her to watch us walk back."

Leigh opened her mouth to answer, but the desk phone rang again. "Fine," she said with a frustrated grunt as she dropped into her chair and snatched up the phone. She waved a hand, and Delilah grabbed my arm and made a run for the front door.

"Geez, are you trying to rip my arm off?" I asked as we burst out the doors.

"I'm trying to get out of there before she hangs up because no one's there," Delilah said, pulling her phone out of her pocket and waving it at me with a grin. I'd never seen her smile before, and I found myself grinning back at her.

Just then, the door behind us opened.

"Oh, shit," I blurted out, taking off for the end of the dorm, the opposite direction of the library.

"Hey," Leigh's voice barked after us. "Where'd you guys go? You're not in the commons!"

I hunkered down beside Delilah at the end of the building, clamping a hand over my mouth to stifle my giggles. Had Leigh seen us?

"What's going on here?" demanded a sharp, female voice.

I let my head thunk against the wall. Damn it. We just had to run while Dr. Rowe was making her rounds.

"Should we make a run for it?" Delilah whispered, her eyes cutting toward the woods. She had weapons. Shit. We'd be in so much trouble if they caught us.

"I let two students go to the library, and I was going to watch them walk, but the phone rang," Leigh explained, sounding a bit desperate. "But they must have gone somewhere else."

The woods were about thirty feet away, across an expanse of lawn. If Dr. Rowe and Leigh were talking, we could sneak over, but if they started sniffing around, as they surely would…

"Who are you looking for?" asked another voice, this one a male voice with the barest hint of an accent.

"That girlfriend of yours," Leigh's voice said with a huff. "She came out here with Delilah, and now they've disappeared."

"Delilah?" Viktor asked. "No, they didn't come out. Maybe they ran up the stairs to see my sister."

"Whatever they're doing, they're up to no good," Dr. Rowe said, her voice sounding closer.

"If they're doing anything together, it's definitely school related," Viktor said. "They can't stand each other."

I glanced at Delilah, my eyes wide, but she'd covered her mouth and was holding back laughter. That made me start giggling with both nerves and relief, and then I had to clamp my own hand over my mouth again.

"I'm calling up to Svana," Leigh said, and the door thudded shut as she went back inside.

"Dr. Rowe, if they came out, they would have gone on this path," Viktor called from the far end of the building, where the main path led to the Ravenwood main building instead of across the lawns.

"What are you doing out here, young man? This is the second time I've found you out under suspicious circumstances."

"I...I was waiting for Timberlyn," Viktor said, sounding chagrined. "That's why I know she didn't come out."

"Come on," I whispered as quietly as I could. "He's creating a diversion."

Delilah and I jumped up and raced on tiptoes toward the woods, which now felt like the safe place instead of the dangerous one. My heart raced just as fast, sure that at any moment, Dr. Rowe's voice would ring out.

Ten feet.

Twenty feet.

Twenty-five. The heavy dew on the grass made my boot slip, and I fell halfway, catching myself on my palm. Delilah grabbed my arm and heaved me up, and we dashed forward again.

And then we were under the shelter of the first tree, scrambling behind the trunk just as the heavy beam of a flashlight swept over the woods. "How do I know you're not protecting them?" Dr. Rowe demanded.

"If I was protecting them, I wouldn't have let them go into the woods," Viktor said.

That's when I saw it, highlighted like a paved trail through the grass. Our footsteps had knocked the dew off the grass, making a clear path to the woods.

"Let's go," I said, grabbing Delilah's arm.

I heard her draw a long, slow breath. "Are you bleeding?"

"What?"

"Make sure you're not bleeding."

I looked down at my palm where I'd caught myself when I slipped. I felt only the tiniest pain, like I'd punctured the skin with a pointy piece of dried grass of pine needle.

"I'm not," I said, wondering why she was asking that. "I'm fine." The tiny mark couldn't have produced more than a single drop of blood. It wasn't like I was leaving a Hansel and Gretel trail for Dr. Rowe to follow.

"Let's go, then," Delilah said, her voice determined now. She crouched low and ran forward between the trees. We had to run in darkness, not daring to turn on our light and catch Dr. Rowe's eye. Luckily, our eyes had adjusted while we hid behind the dorm, and the moonlight kept us from running into any tree trunks. We dodged around pines and scrambled over rocks, heading in the direction that I was almost sure led to the tiny wooden shack.

It had been a long time, though. It had taken me too long to ponder where it was, to get my courage up, to find someone to back me up. Every statistic out there said she was probably dead by now. Though the thought made me sick, I tried to accept it. Still, I wasn't going to let percentages stop me. If there was even a chance that she was alive, it was worth continuing.

After a while, we stopped running. I tried to get my bearings, to figure out where we were and which direction we needed to go. I was pretty sure of the general direction, but the longer we stayed on a wrong trail, the later it would get. I knew the wolves visited Grandma's just after her bedtime, which wasn't long after dark. We'd already passed that. Would they be coming back this way already?

Counting on my keen sense of direction, we veered a bit to the left and continued at a brisk walk.

"Did you really only hate me all this time because you think I like Alarick?" I asked.

"Let's not talk," Delilah said. "Remember the whole not-friends thing?"

"Oh, okay," I said, disappointed by her answer. Not only because I couldn't ever leave well enough alone, but because I'd thought maybe we were on the road to friendship despite what she'd said. We'd run from the dean, laughing together at the thrill of escape. That kind of thing could make friends out of complete strangers, and we weren't exactly strangers. We'd been living together for six months now.

We walked in silence for a while, until I felt a crawling sensation creeping across my skin. It wasn't the tingle of Alarick's presence, either. It was a cold, damp presence that gripped my heart in an iron fist and wouldn't let me draw a breath.

"What the hell is that?" Delilah asked, stopping dead in her tracks.

"What?" I asked. It was a moment before I saw what she saw, the thing I felt. My heart stopped. A dark, formless black swirled in front of us, and inside it glowed a pair of white eyes without pupils.

My dream. I knew it was the thing from my nightmare even before the smell of wet fur and rotting oranges choked my throat. My feet were frozen to the ground.

Delilah coughed, covering her mouth with her arm and backing away. She swore, yanking at something on her belt as the shadow advanced, towering over us, spreading wider like a mouth about to swallow us.

"Run," I croaked. But Delilah had other plans. She yanked a knife free and hurled it at the creature. Instead of striking with a thud, the knife disappeared into the blackness as if it had been swallowed up by a black hole.

A shriek sounded, so shrill it felt like needles had punctured my eardrums. I clamped my hands to my ears, wanting to curl up in a ball and hide my head. But the thing began to separate, and I remembered those pieces of it devouring my wolf in my dream.

"Run," I screamed, my voice loud and clear this time. I grabbed Delilah's arm, and we took off. But in a second, she was the one dragging me. I lost my footing, but she didn't stop. She shot through the woods faster than anyone could run, the trees blurring beside us. She was…carrying me, running so fast my body was whipping straight out behind her.

Fuck. She must be one of them, a werewolf, too. There was no way a human could run that fast, could move that fast. But the shadow could. It was right behind us, moving even faster, closing in by the second.

Chapter Twenty-One

"The light," I screamed. "Give me the flashlight."

"What?"

"The light drives away monsters," I said, frantically grabbing at her pocket. It was a thing my grandmother had taught me when I was young, and I'd had a nightmare at her house. It was something I'd been practicing for years. It always worked.

Delilah fumbled for the light, and I snatched it out of her hands, my fingers shaking as I hit the switch. A beam of harsh, LED light streamed from the muzzle of the flashlight, piercing the darkness. The ear-piercing shrieks resumed, echoing through the woods, but instead of charging at us, the creature flailed. Pieces of it ripped free, and it writhed as if in pain.

"It's dying," Delilah said, taking off again.

"No," I yelled, stomping my feet down hard. "It's not gone yet!"

My feet hit something hard, and my arm felt like it was wrenched from the socket as Delilah continued, still gripping me. The shadow creature was still disintegrating, and I tried to keep the beam on it, but the next second, we were hurtling forward, tumbling down a steep incline. Roots and rocks tore at us as we tumbled head over feet, our limbs twisting and our bodies jarring against the embankment until we slammed to a stop at the bottom.

It took me a good five minutes to recover from the multiple blows to the head I'd received in the fall. I finally looked around to find Delilah crouching a little way off, her face in her hands.

"You okay?" I asked, putting weight on my hand to see if I could sit.

"What the hell was that?" she asked.

"I don't know," I said. "A monster from one of my dreams."

"You summoned that thing?" she asked, lifting her head.

"Not intentionally," I said.

"How'd you know what to do to get rid of it?"

"I… I didn't," I admitted, pushing myself to an upright position. "I just did what I do when it appears in my nightmares. My grandma always says light will chase away the darkness and the monsters that come with it."

Delilah shuddered. "I thought you were… I don't know… *Normal.* What are you?"

"A little nuts, maybe," I said with a shaky laugh. "I think the better question is, what are you?"

Delilah looked up at the walls of the steep ravine we'd fallen into. "Actually, I think the better question is, where are we, and how do we get out of here before that thing comes back?"

I couldn't answer any of those questions. I started feeling around in the rocks and rubble for the flashlight. The walls were too steep to climb, and I definitely hadn't been here before. I'd heard all about hikers falling into ravines, but I hadn't seen a single one in these woods until tonight. When I came up empty handed, I sat back against the rocky wall with a sigh. My head was throbbing, and my whole body felt like it had been through a battle.

I searched my pockets, but my phone had fallen out, too.

"Do you have your phone?" I asked. "We could call emergency rescue or something."

Delilah pulled out a phone and flicked it on. "No service down here," she said.

"We could yell for help and hope that someone friendly finds us," I said, though I didn't think anything friendly would be on this property. I thought about slimy Mr. Wolf, and how Alarick said anything on his property was his. Yeah, I didn't think yelling was such a good idea. Alarick might have saved me once, but I didn't know if he'd do it again. Especially not if Delilah got stabbity when she saw them.

"I have a flare," Delilah. "I'm sure we're already going to be drawing creatures because of all our cuts and scratches. They'll smell the blood. At least this way, someone else might find us first. It's better than screaming ourselves silly."

"You brought a flare?"

She shrugged. "I figured if the Wolf guys wanted to kill us, at least I could go down swinging. Leave a mark for someone to find me."

She turned away as she spoke, kneeling on the ground. After a minute of muttering under her breath, she stood up and threw something into the air. A spire of blue sparks shot a hundred feet into the air, high above the ravine, as sparkling and beautiful as fireworks. It didn't look like any kind of flare I'd ever seen, not that I'd seen many. Maybe it was a Canadian flare. Or maybe it was some kind of… I felt stupid just having the thought, but the word that came to mind was *magic*. But I already knew Delilah wasn't normal, as she'd called me.

"Interesting flare," I said.

"Thanks," she said, brushing off her hands.

"You know what the Wolf boys are," I said slowly. "Don't you?"

"I don't know what you mean."

"Are you one of them?" I asked.

"Do I look like one of them?"

"No," I admitted. "But neither does Brooklyn."

Delilah crossed her arms. "Doesn't she? She hangs out with them."

Before I could point out the holes in that argument, I heard a voice from above. "Timberlyn? Is that you?"

Relief coursed through me, and I almost sagged against Delilah. "Yeah."

"I knew you couldn't just forget about it," Svana called down. "I can't believe you tried to ditch us. Viktor told me what happened as soon as Dr. Rowe left, and we tried to follow you. We've been looking for hours. What was that signal you just sent?"

"A flare," Delilah said, sounding a bit defensive.

"Nice," Viktor called down. "How do you want us to get you out?"

"Did you happen to bring any rope along with that flare?" I asked Delilah.

"Very funny," she said.

"Rope ladder?" I said. "We can tie our clothes together."

"Not exactly the moment I wanted Viktor to see me naked," Delilah muttered.

"Do you have a better idea?"

We stripped down to our undergarments and threw our clothes up, weighted with rocks to help them get momentum. Within half an hour, we'd made a rope of all our clothes, and those above us lowered it down. Still, it dangled at least ten feet up from our fingertips."

"Got any superpowers that can help with this?" I asked Delilah.

"Don't be a twat."

"There's a log up here we can push down, if you can climb that to get up to the rope," Svana called.

"Stand back so it doesn't hit you," Viktor called.

A few minutes later, what looked like an entire tree appeared over the ravine.

"Timber," Svana yelled, and the giant log began to topple and bounce down the wall of the ravine. It was far from us, but I could feel the ground tremble as it tumbled down with giant thuds, crashes, and cracks. Rocks and branches snapped, and I couldn't help but think there was no way everyone in a five-mile radius hadn't heard that.

I thought the log was going to fall along the bottom of the ravine, but at the last minute, it seemed to hang suspended, and then decided to fall conveniently propped against the side of the ravine. I gave Delilah some serious side-eye. "Finally a bit of luck?"

"Right?" she said with a little grin.

"You know I'm not going to stop until you tell me."

"Tell you what?" she asked, striding past me and scrambling up the log.

Viktor had moved to the spot above the log, and when the rope ladder came down this time, Delilah grabbed it and scrambled up. I climbed after her, not nearly as quickly. Her petite form was deceptively strong. Unnaturally strong.

But I knew we didn't have time to argue right now. The Wolf boys would be here any minute, coming to see what all the noise was about. And the blood. Could they really smell that? Would they know it was me if they found the scent? I might not have been leaving a trail back at the dorm, but I was now. I had dozens of scrapes and cuts all over my body along with the bruises and a throbbing skull, and Delilah didn't look any better.

"I can't believe you guys came," I said, hugging Svana while Delilah let Viktor check her injuries. She gave me a giddy grin behind his back that made me happy that nothing had ever happened between me and him.

"Are you here to convince us to go back?" I asked. "Because it's a little late."

"Nope," Svana said. "You know what, if you believe what you believe, then that's good enough for us. We'll help you find whatever you're looking for."

A swell of emotion rose inside me, strangling any words I might have said. I had friends. Real friends, who would do anything for me, who were down for anything I could cook up. I didn't deserve it, and yet, why didn't I? I hadn't done much to earn their friendship, but so what? Despite our differences and little spats, we'd treated each other with kindness and respect, and that's what had made us friends. Not because any of us had performed some grand gesture to prove we were worthy of each other's friendship.

"I don't think anything's broken," Viktor pronounced, stepping back from Delilah.

"Okay, let's get dressed and get our bearings," I said, pulling up the rope of clothes.

"Good luck with that," Svana said. "We'd never have found you without the flare."

"I'm pretty sure I can figure it out," I said. We quickly dressed, and then I stood there looking at all the trees, at the ravine, at the position of the moon. It was past midnight, and it had started its descent, which made things easier. I oriented myself by its direction, which let me know the four cardinal directions. From there, I could find the general direction of Ravenwood, Grandma's house, and the shack. "Got it," I said, starting off. I'd turned my ankle, and every step I took felt like fire. Still, we'd survived, and my friends were here. If we could find the shack, we could still get out of there before morning.

I traced our steps and found the place where we'd run from the shadows. That's where we had gone wrong. From there, I turned toward the place I remembered the shack. About twenty minutes later, I stepped onto bare dirt instead of pine needles, and my heart lurched into my throat.

"This is it," I said, pulling up short. "This is the path to the shack."

As we got closer, I grew more and more certain. This was it. My knees began to shake. What if we were too late? What if we found Amy's body? Or nothing at all?

What if we found her, and she was as unhinged as Brooklyn?

Suddenly, the hair on the back of my neck prickled, and a hot shiver rushed over my skin.

"They're here," I whispered, hurrying even faster.

"Who?" asked Delilah.

"The wolves," Viktor muttered through clenched teeth.

Delilah shot me a look. "How do you know?"

I didn't have time to answer, though. A growl sounded in the woods beside us, and a soft padding footstep sounded. The next moment, an enormous wolf slid from the shadows and into the path in front of us.

I swore under my breath and stopped walking. Delilah shrank against Viktor. "Got any other superpowers that would help us out right about now?" she hissed.

"We're going to that cabin," I told Alarick. "You can't stop us."

He growled in response.

My heart hammered in my ears, but I held my ground. "You picked the wrong girl to mess with when you took Amy. If you didn't want me involved, you shouldn't have taken my friend."

He snarled again, this time tilting his head toward the woods. The next second, two move wolves appeared to either side of us, and the next, two more flanked us. Delilah hid her face in Viktor's shoulder. "What now?" Svana asked, crowding in with them.

Now we should turn and go back, I thought. They had us surrounded. But we weren't going back. This was the last full moon before the school year ended. It had to be tonight.

"Now we fight," Viktor said quietly.

"Ride or die," Delilah whispered, holding up a fist. Too bad she had already thrown her knife away on the shadow monster, and I didn't even have a phone. Not that a puny little cell phone would do anything but bounce off the forehead of one of the enormous wolves. They closed in on us, growling, and for the first time in a while, I was really scared of them. They may have been human in their other form, but in this form, they were animals. I didn't know how much humanity they retained. And they didn't look happy to have four intruders so close.

"Don't follow me," Svana whispered.

"What?" I hissed back.

Without answering, Svana bolted. I swallowed a scream as two of the wolves turned and raced after her.

Viktor's hand closed around mine, strong but gentle, his back pressed to mine. "She'll be okay. She's just giving us a better chance."

"She'll be okay?" I asked, my voice quavering. "How will she be okay?"

And how was this a better chance? Four enormous wolves against three defenseless humans. I couldn't think my way out of this one. The wolves in my dreams were my friends. They weren't chased away by light or anything else. They stood their ground and gazed at me with sadness and wisdom in their eyes. These wolves gnashed their teeth and snarled at us.

"Delilah," Viktor said. "Are you ready?"

"Yeah, sure, I'm totally ready to die," she muttered. "I mean, I've already lived almost eighteen years. What more could I ask for?"

I was glad to know I wasn't the only one freaking out. Viktor sounded so normal. If he was afraid, he wasn't showing it. I found Delilah's hand and gave it a squeeze. We might not have been friends, but we were about to die together, and that somehow made everything else meaningless. Whatever flare-throwing and racing abilities she had, her supernatural skills didn't seem to extend to fighting giant wolves.

"What do they want?" I whispered.

"To rip our faces off?" Delilah guessed. As if to prove her right, one of the wolves dove at us. Viktor leapt away from us, into its path. This time, the scream tore from my throat as the wolf flattened my friend and another jumped onto them. One of the other wolves leapt at us.

"Run," Delilah screamed, darting from one side to the other as the wolf lunged at her. "They won't kill you. Get Amy!" The wolf hit her at last, pinning her under it. I screamed and leapt at it, but it was too late. Though I pounded it with fists and feet, it didn't seem to notice as its teeth clamped down on Delilah's shoulder. She shrieked like a banshee, unintelligible curses streaming from her mouth.

A thud sounded behind me, and I saw one of the wolves lying folded around the base of a tree. My head whipped around, trying to find whatever had thrown the enormous wolf, but all I saw was Viktor fighting with one wolf, and the other just standing there staring at me.

My wolf.

As I watched, he crumpled to the ground. I lurched forward, but before I'd even reached him, the other wolves had collapsed all around the clearing. Viktor lay motionless halfway under one of the wolves. I stood frozen, torn between running to my friend and my wolf.

"Timberlyn," Delilah rasped. I spun to find her still lying on the ground, her shoulder mangled beyond recognition and blood spreading across the pine needles under her.

I ran over and dropped to my knees at her side. "What can I do?" I asked.

Her eyes were glassy and unfocused, and the sight made me almost lose it. "Get Amy," she said, her hand groping for mine.

I grabbed it and held on tight, squeezing her fingers as if I could make her hold on longer. "You're not going to die," I said, forcing my voice out steady. "I'm going to wrap your shoulder, and you're going to be just fine."

"They won't be out for long," she said. "Go now."

"I don't want to leave you," I whispered. "She might be dead already."

"Here," she said, lifting her leather vest. Only then did I see the pistol tucked into her belt. I had no idea where that had been all this time. Why hadn't she used it to save herself?

"I can't take it," I said, the lump in my throat making my voice a croak.

"It's only got one shot left," she said. "And it's too late for me to use it. You know how?"

"I'm from Arkansas," I said, swiping a tear from my cheek. "Yeah, I know how."

Delilah's eyes fell closed. "Go," she whispered. "Hurry."

I swallowed back a sob, and an argument, and all the things I wanted to say to her. Taking out the gun, I stood and glanced around at the wolves, who apparently weren't dead, and Viktor, who I wasn't sure about. I wanted nothing more than to lay down with them, but there was no time to cry. I took a deep breath, glanced around one last time, and took off for the shack.

Chapter Twenty-Two

As I jogged up the trail, I forced my mind to remain calm and blank. I had to get Amy, or this was all for nothing. Far too high a price had already been paid for her freedom—Delilah's life, maybe Viktor's, Svana's, and even some of the wolves'. If I failed now, every death and injury was on my hands. Which meant there would be no failing.

I reached the cabin in a few minutes. It was as dark as I remembered, and no moonlight hit the small window. The moon was sinking, and the slightest bit of light was coming into the sky in the east. I should have been exhausted, but a cold calm had gripped me. I found the padlock still in place, as expected. I gave it a yank, anyway. I didn't want to waste my one bullet on the padlock, so I stuck the gun in my belt and grabbed a nearby rock, which I used to smash the window. I struggled through the window and landed inside with a thud of my boots on the floor.

For a second, I couldn't see anything.

"Amy?" I whispered.

"Looking for something?" a voice asked from the darkness.

I cried out in shock and stumbled backward against the wall. A light flared, and I blinked to see past the bright flame that had appeared in an old-fashioned kerosene lantern.

"Mr. Wolf," I said, my heart slamming against my ribcage like it would tear its way free. My eyes darted around the room, landing on a narrow bed behind the hulking figure. A slender shape lay under a thin blanket. I nearly collapsed with relief. She was here, just as I'd thought.

And so was the last person on earth I wanted to see, sitting at a tiny, round table with a lantern and a cigar box in front of him.

"Don't look so shocked," he said, his voice an oily purr. "You're on my property, Ginger."

"That's not my name."

He shrugged one shoulder almost imperceptibly. "Glad you made it. Looks like my sons brought me a fresh one for tonight after all."

"What?" My heart thundered in my ears so loud I didn't know if I'd hear an answer. It couldn't be true. They had tried to stop me from coming here to find Amy. They hadn't driven me here.

Mr. Wolf gestured vaguely to the twin bed behind him. "I'm afraid my sons don't always approve of this project. I wasn't sure anything I said could convince them to bring me another one after the unfortunate end of the last one."

"Oh, so they're not on board with kidnapping random girls?" I asked, but my mind was focused on what he'd said about the last one. Did that mean Amy was dead?

Mr. Wolf gave an unimpressed chuckle. "Not random," he said. "Human girls."

"Why?" I demanded. "What did those girls ever do to you?"

"It's not a question of what they did to me," he said, taking out a cigar and sliding it from the plastic wrapper. "It's a question of what they can do for me."

I shuddered at the thought of what he might have done to my friend. "I'm here to get Amy back," I said. "That's all."

Mr. Wolf chuckled again, fitting the end of the cigar in a cutter and slicing it off. "That's not all, Miss Brink," he said. "I've got big plans for you."

"You know who I am."

He gave a snort that heaved his heavy body as he lit his cigar. "Of course I know who you are," he said. "I know all the human girls at Ravenwood. You think you're special enough to attend a school like that without a gift?

Everyone is at Ravenwood for a reason. You're there to serve my sons. Didn't they tell you?"

I gritted my teeth against the words I wanted to say to him—to scream at him. I needed to keep him talking until I figured out how to get my gun out and fire it without him stopping me.

"If I'm here to serve your sons, what is everyone else here for?"

"To master their gifts," he said. "But I'm not interested in them. That's Dr. Underwood's project."

"So, he lets you lure human girls here to change into werewolves," I said. "Meanwhile, he's recruiting… Non-humans?"

"Exactly," Mr. Wolf said. "You humans are supposed to be kept in the dark, but I understand you caught on to something going on. We usually try to test the humans for compatibility earlier in the year in case they get suspicious. We've had a time with our successful candidate, though."

"Her name is Brooklyn."

He did that tiny shrug again, as if even the girl whose life he had changed forever, who he had made into his species, was no more important to him than a human, though from his tone, he held no regard whatsoever for humans.

"There were only four human girls at Ravenwood?" I asked, suddenly feeling a sick sense of betrayal. I'd been there six months, and I was the last human they were going to pick off.

"Four new ones," he said. "There are others who have been here longer."

"The other girls who disappeared," I whispered. But my mind was on the last words he'd said. New this year. That meant my friends might be human. They might. Maybe they didn't know, and they hadn't intentionally made me believe I was crazy when I told them about the werewolves. Maybe they hadn't been lying to me all along.

Or maybe they had. Maybe their was a reason they were inhumanly beautiful, and didn't eat, and had been able to throw an entire freaking tree into the ravine to get us out.

"Doesn't matter now," Mr. Wolf said, leaning back and crossing an ankle over his knee. He let out a puff of sweet-smelling smoke. "You're here, you're human. You want to be a Wolf. That's why you came, isn't it?"

I couldn't tell if he was talking about his family or the animal, but his boasting tone said it was the first. Either way, I had an honest answer to that question.

"Not interested," I said, fighting the urge to cross my arms and glare at him. I needed my hand. It was sneaking closer to my belt every moment.

"I'm afraid you don't have much of a choice," Mr. Wolf said, puffing on his cigar and smirking at me like this was all very entertaining. "My sons need a mate, and you're a viable candidate."

"Excuse me?" I asked, gulping over my words and trying not to sound as alarmed as I felt.

"What do you think we need a mere human for?" he said. "You see, werewolves are all but extinct. In fact, my sons are some of the last naturally born wolves in existence. But in order for them to pass on our bloodline, we must create female mates for them."

"That's what you're kidnapping girls for?" I asked, even more horrified than I'd been when I thought he was just a regular girl-snatching psycho.

"If humanity was in danger, wouldn't you want to save your species?"

"Yeah, but not like this." I gestured to the shape in the bed behind him. My eyes narrowed when I studied it. "Is that Amy? Or Nancy? Where's the other one?"

"Making a human into a wolf isn't an exact science," he said. "It's a long process to train a new wolf. If Brooklyn hadn't gotten away while hunting, we wouldn't have reintroduced her into the school so soon. But there will always be sacrifices. That's the cost of doing things for the greater good."

"The greater good of who?" I asked. "Not these girls you're *sacrificing.*"

"As I said, for the good of our race. And you can wipe that self-righteous look off your face, Ginger. Don't you study history? Your race didn't hesitate to drive wild wolves to near extinction for simply threatening your livestock. Is it so much to risk a few lives so that my species can go on?"

"Ask that to Amy," I said.

Mr. Wolf puffed on his cigar and then set it down. "You wanted a chance to start over, didn't you? Did you have such a bad year at Ravenwood? You made friends. You weren't an outcast."

My throat tightened as I stared at him. "How do you know any of that?"

"My sons and their friends have spent their time at Ravenwood on a very special project," he said. "They've found lots of people like you, Ginger. You don't think you're the only outcast suffering in a public school, do you?"

"No, but..."

"They've tracked down lots of girls like you. Ones who don't quite fit. You see, we think sometimes this is a product of a human's unique abilities. As you know, your kind likes to single out those who are extraordinary in ways they don't understand. We've given you a place here where you fit. Where your gifts might even make you an ideal candidate for making the change to werewolf."

I swallowed hard, sliding my hand ever so slowly up the wall, toward my hip. "You're the one who sent the letter? Who invited me here?"

"Of course," he said, leaning forward and then standing from his chair, his huge frame seeming to fill the whole room. "You didn't think Dr. Underwood was responsible, did you? That bumbling idiot couldn't find his own feet if I wasn't here to point them out."

"You invited me here to change me into a wolf?" I asked. "You've been planning this all along?"

"Exactly," he said. "And just like the other girls, you made it far too easy. You even came right to me. The others had to be lured by the promise of my boys' love, but you came right to my doorstep."

"That's sick," I burst out. But what I was thinking was that the boys hadn't lured me. They'd warned me, tried to chase me away. All along, they'd been trying to stop this from happening. Alarick had tried to keep me from this fate, from his father. And instead of listening to them, I'd walked right into the trap.

"Call it what you like," Mr. Wolf said. "It's a necessity. Only one of the four candidates this year has taken. And of course we won't know if she's capable of bearing a werewolf child for a few years yet. We can't risk stopping with just one."

"You won't get away with this."

"I already have," he said, advancing on me.

"Don't hurt me," I whimpered, cowering against the wall so I could turn and obscure the gun.

"Think again," growled a familiar voice from outside. Running footsteps sounded, and a heavy blow hit the door. It was just the distraction I needed.

I snatched for the pistol, pulling it out and clicking the safety off in one swift movement.

But I wasn't fast enough.

Mr. Wolf lunged, quick as a snake striking. His hand closed around mine, twisting it backward just as the door burst inward with a splintering crash. Mr. Wolf lunged forward and sank his teeth into the side of my neck. I let out a cry of pain, my whole body tensing reflexively. My hand clenched, and my finger squeezed the trigger.

A single, deafening shot sounded.

In the doorway behind me, a body fell.

LENA MAE HILL

Printed in Great Britain
by Amazon

18393171R00181